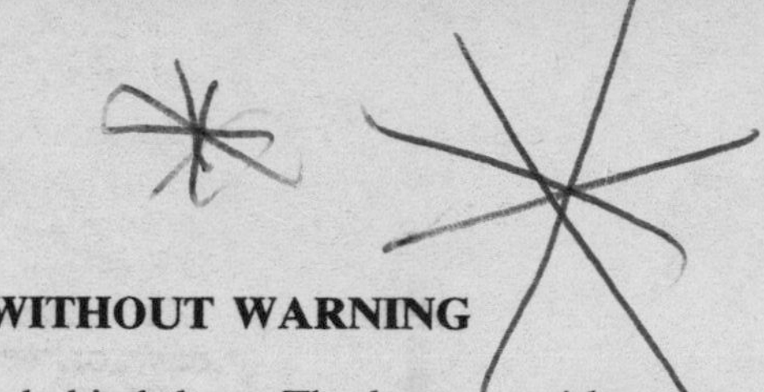

WITHOUT WARNING

Fargo glided up behind them. The last man either sensed or heard him and began to turn. Fargo did not tell him to drop his knife. He did not call on them to give up or shout for help. He simply stepped in close and buried his toothpick to the hilt in the seaman's back.

The would-be murderer bent like a bow and his mouth opened wide, but all he did was gasp. Then his eyes glazed and his legs buckled and he collapsed in a dead heap.

The gasp had been enough, though. The man in front of him heard it, and whirled. With a sharp bark of anger, the man attacked, cleaving the air with a big knife. . . .

ALASKAN VENGEANCE

by

Jon Sharpe

A SIGNET BOOK

SIGNET
Published by New American Library, a division of
Penguin Group (USA) Inc., 375 Hudson Street,
New York, New York 10014, USA
Penguin Group (Canada), 90 Eglinton Avenue East, Suite 700, Toronto,
Ontario M4P 2Y3, Canada (a division of Pearson Penguin Canada Inc.)
Penguin Books Ltd., 80 Strand, London WC2R 0RL, England
Penguin Ireland, 25 St. Stephen's Green, Dublin 2,
Ireland (a division of Penguin Books Ltd.)
Penguin Group (Australia), 250 Camberwell Road, Camberwell, Victoria 3124,
Australia (a division of Pearson Australia Group Pty. Ltd.)
Penguin Books India Pvt. Ltd., 11 Community Centre, Panchsheel Park,
New Delhi - 110 017, India
Penguin Group (NZ), 67 Apollo Drive, Rosedale, North Shore 0745,
Auckland, New Zealand (a division of Pearson New Zealand Ltd.)
Penguin Books (South Africa) (Pty.) Ltd., 24 Sturdee Avenue,
Rosebank, Johannesburg 2196, South Africa

Penguin Books Ltd., Registered Offices:
80 Strand, London WC2R 0RL, England

First published by Signet, an imprint of New American Library,
a division of Penguin Group (USA) Inc.

First Printing, August 2007
10 9 8 7 6 5 4 3 2 1

The first chapter of this book previously appeared in *California Carnage*, the three hundred ninth volume in this series.

 REGISTERED TRADEMARK—MARCA REGISTRADA

Printed in the United States of America

The Trailsman

Beginnings . . . they bend the tree and they mark the man. Skye Fargo was born when he was eighteen. Terror was his midwife, vengeance his first cry. Killing spawned Skye Fargo, ruthless, cold-blooded murder. Out of the acrid smoke of gunpowder still hanging in the air, he rose, cried out a promise never forgotten.

The Trailsman they began to call him all across the West: searcher, scout, hunter, the man who could see where others only looked, his skills for hire but not his soul, the man who lived each day to the fullest, yet trailed each tomorrow. Skye Fargo, the Trailsman, the seeker who could take the wildness of a land and the wanting of a woman and make them his own.

Alaska, 1861—where old hatreds snare the unwary in a web of deceit and bloodshed.

1

Skye Fargo did not like being taken for a fool. He did not like it at all.

Dawn found him winding down a hill below a sawmill. A big man, broad of shoulder and slender of hip, he wore buckskins, a white hat brown with dust, and a faded red bandanna. A Colt with well-worn grips was at his waist. Piercing blue eyes surveyed the scene below.

At the docks a schooner was making ready to leave, her crew scurrying to hoist sails and lift anchor. Scores of seagulls engaged in aerial acrobatics out over the bay, their raucous cries rising to the few fluffy clouds in the blue sky. A large fish jumped, too far off for Fargo to tell what kind it was, making a tremendous splash.

Fargo liked Seattle. It was not as worldly and sophisticated as New Orleans or as wild and woolly as Denver, but it had a rustic charm those cities lacked. Already, though, that charm was being taxed by business interests out to turn quaint Seattle into a bustling seaport.

Those interests accounted for the hotels that had sprung up along the waterfront. Only three so far, the best being the Royale. The other two catered to patrons with more modest means.

Fargo went to each in turn and inquired at the front desk. Did they have someone named Frank Toomey staying there? The clerk at the Shanty checked the register and said that they did. "Mr. Toomey is in room twenty-seven. Go down this hall to your right and turn left when you come to the end. His room is the third on the right."

The hall smelled of the sea and less pleasant odors. Fargo knocked twice but received no answer. About to knock again, he tried the latch on an impulse. The door creaked as it swung open.

"Toomey?" Fargo said, poking his head inside.

The smell was worse. A lot of it had to do with the blood that had pooled under Frank Toomey's wrists. Near the old man lay an open razor.

"Damn." Fargo sprang to the man's side and sank to one knee. Quickly, he felt for a pulse and found one. A weak one, but Toomey was still alive. How long he would remain that way was anyone's guess. There was a terrible lot of blood.

The desk clerk was scribbling in a ledger when Fargo flew into the lobby. "You need to fetch a sawbones. The man in twenty-seven slit his wrists."

"He did what?" the clerk asked in disbelief. "Are you sure? Maybe I should take a look."

Reaching across the counter, Fargo grabbed him by the front of his shirt. "Am I sure? What kind of stupid question is that? Get a doctor and get one fast or the gent in twenty-seven won't be the only one who needs one."

"But I'm not supposed to leave the front desk unattended," the young man complained.

Fargo's temper flared. "Were you born a jackass or have you worked at it?" Extending his other arm, he hauled the clerk up and over the counter and practically threw him to the floor. Several onlookers gasped but Fargo didn't care.

"A doctor!" he bellowed, and planted the tip of his boot on a sensitive part of the clerk's anatomy.

Scrambling upright, the young man fled as if his life were in peril.

Fargo hurried back to the room. He had left the door open and someone had seen Toomey and the blood, and now half a dozen gawkers blocked the doorway. He shouldered through them, none too gently, and discovered a gray-haired bag of bones with Toomey's head in his lap. "Is he still alive?"

"Barely," the man said sadly.

"Do you know him?" Fargo asked.

"Barely," the man said again. "I'm in the next room. Nestor Willis is my name. We talked a little yesterday when he got here and again for a few minutes last night after he came back from playing cards."

Fargo gestured at the scarlet pools. "Any idea why he took that razor to his veins?"

"He was awful upset," Nestor said. "He wouldn't say why but I gathered it had something to do with him losing something that meant everything to him. His exact words."

Fargo thought of the claim to the mine, and scowled.

"I never thought he would do something like this," Nestor said. "He was a nice guy. Kept saying as how he was going to do right by his kids and grandkids and give them more money than they would know what to do with." Nestor had to stop and cough to clear his throat. "I got the impression he really loved them."

"He's not buried yet," Fargo said.

"What? Oh. Sorry. There's just so much blood, and his pulse is so weak." Nestor bowed his head. "Why does it always have to be like this? Why can't it leave us be?"

"What?"

"Life," Nestor said. "Why does it always batter us down and leave us worse off than when we came into the world?"

"You're asking the wrong person," Fargo said. He had stopped looking for answers about the time it dawned on him that life was a roll of the dice, and the dice were rigged.

"Don't you ever wish things were different?" Nestor asked. "Don't you ever wish we were happy and healthy our whole lives long?"

"I have never been all that interested in fairy tales," Fargo remarked.

Nestor mustered a wan smile. "It just never made any sense to me, is all. Toomey, here, told me I was too gloomy for my own good. Imagine. Him saying that about me, yet he's the one who goes and cuts himself to end it all. People sure are peculiar."

"You can say that again."

At that moment shoes pounded in the hall and the gawkers parted to admit the out-of-breath desk clerk and a middle-aged man in a rumpled suit, carrying a black bag.

"I'm Dr. James," was all the physician said. He hastily took a stethoscope from his bag and listened to Toomey's chest, then examined both wrists, and grunted. "There is hope. Not much, but some." He pointed at the clerk. "Find six men to help carry him. Then remove the door and we will use it as a stretcher."

"Carry him where?" the desk clerk inquired.

"Out front, of course. I will have a carriage brought. I must stitch him but I would rather do it at my office, where my equipment is handy and I won't have the curious breathing down my neck."

The desk clerk took the hint. He dispersed the gawkers, except for two husky men, and found two more elsewhere. Fargo and Nestor Willis made six. The clerk ran up front for the hotel's toolbox, and it was Fargo who undid the hinges so the door could be lowered and Toomey carefully placed on top of it.

Dr. James was ready with a blanket. He covered Toomey to his chin and gestured. "Off you go. And for God's sake, don't drop him. This man is hanging to life by a thread."

No one spoke. Most of the bearers would not look at Toomey. They walked as if they were stepping on eggshells and dared not break one.

A carriage was waiting. The physician's own carriage. There was not enough room for the door so they carefully lifted Toomey up and just as carefully laid him down on the rear seat. The doctor gave hurried instructions to the driver, then surprised Fargo by turning to him and saying, "I would like you to accompany us, if you don't mind."

"What good would I be?"

"The desk clerk told me that you know this man," Dr. James said. "If I can restore him it would be nice to have someone he knows standing by when he comes around."

Fargo opened his mouth to say that he hardly knew the man, and changed his mind. He climbed in.

The driver went as fast as was prudent. Twice the doctor yelled up for him to slow down. In due course the driver brought the carriage to a stop in front of a log and stone building.

The physician's office was on the first floor. The driver helped them carry Frank Toomey inside and place him on a long table. Dr. James immediately set to work. First he laid out the items he would need: a long needle, much like a sewing needle only the sharp end had a slight curve; a pair of surgical scissors; and the thread he would use to sew the cut flesh. "You can wait outside if you want," he said to Fargo.

"I'm not squeamish."

The stitching up took about half an hour. Dr. James worked quickly, and efficiently, and when he was done, he stepped back and mopped his brow with his sleeve. "That's all I can do. His life is in higher hands than mine."

"Will he make it?" Fargo asked.

"Hard to say," the sawbones admitted. "He has lost a lot of blood. Perhaps too much to live."

"Is there any way to replace it?"

"Not that I know of, no," the physician replied while replacing the curved needle and the scissors in his surgical kit. "Oh, there have been a few reports from Europe where the blood of one person has been introduced into the veins of another. Transfusions, they're called. But most of the recipients died. I wouldn't want to chance it." He thoughtfully regarded Toomey. "The theory is sound. But it doesn't work like it should. The best medical men have worked on it but no one has any idea why."

"Maybe all blood isn't the same," Fargo speculated. It made sense to him. No two people were ever exactly alike, so why should their blood be any different?

Dr. James smiled. "A quaint notion, but blood is blood. No, it has to be something else. In any event, I am not about to risk giving Mr. Toomey a transfusion when it very well might kill him." He made for the door. "I will be back in a while to check on him. In the meantime, if you could stay and watch over him, I would be grateful."

"I'll stay," Fargo said. He had his reasons, which had nothing to do with the health of the patient. Pulling out a chair, he propped his boots on the operating table and settled down to wait.

The doctor had been gone about an hour when Frank Toomey groaned and stirred. His eyelids fluttered but he did not open them for another five minutes. He gazed about the room in dazed confusion until his eyes found Fargo. Then he licked his lips and said weakly, "You."

"We have to talk."

"Where am I?" Toomey asked. "Why am I still alive? I thought for sure I did myself in."

"You are at a doctor's office," Fargo enlightened him. "He's stitched you up but you still might have your way."

"Good." Toomey sounded relieved. "I want to get it over with. I have nothing to live for now that I've lost my claim."

"That's what I want to talk about," Fargo said. "You hoodwinked me, you old goat."

Toomey was struggling to stay conscious. "I beg your pardon? I wagered my claim in good faith in that poker game. You won the claim fairly."

"This is the United States of America, not Russia," Fargo said.

"Yes. So?"

"So your precious claim is in Alaska, and Alaska is Russian territory. You were clever in forging the claim, but you made the mistake of writing it in English. It should be in Russian." Fargo was proud of his deduction. Most people would not have caught on.

A sound that was not quite a laugh and not quite a gurgle bubbled from Frank Toomey's throat. "You don't know much about Alaska, do you?"

"I've never been there," Fargo admitted.

Toomey swallowed a couple of times, then said quietly, "If you had been, you would know that Alaska has been run by the Russian-American Company for over sixty years. The Russian government wants nothing to do with it."

"How does that affect your claim?"

"It's not my claim any longer—it's yours," Toomey replied. "And what it means is that there are a lot of Americans up there. English is spoken as much as Russian. It is not unusual for a document like a claim to be drawn up in English if the person who owns the claim is American."

"Then it's real?"

"Haven't you been paying attention? I told you that at the start. Yes, the claim is real. The Russian-American Company will honor it as they would any other legal document. You really and truly won the right to dig up however much gold as is there."

"I'll be damned," Fargo said.

"Is that why you looked me up? You wanted to call me a liar to my face?"

Fargo did not say anything. He did not need to.

"You are a hard man, mister," Frank Toomey said. "But you can rest easy. Take the next ship to Sitka and soon you will be rolling in riches." Toomey went to say more but passed out, his chin lolling on his chest.

Sliding his boots off the operating table, Fargo stood. He pressed his fingers to Toomey's wrist, then went to the outer office. No one was there. The physician had gone off somewhere.

With a sigh, Fargo went back into the other room. He stood staring out the window for the longest while, until once again Frank Toomey groaned and opened his eyes. Fargo went and stood over him.

"You're still here?" Toomey croaked. "I figured you would be packing for your trip."

"What's this I hear about your kids and grandkids?"

Toomey's face lit like the sun. "You must have been talking to Nestor. I have a son and a daughter, both married, and six grandchildren. We have never had much money. Hand to mouth, year in and year out, that's always how it has been. My strike could have changed that."

"Yet you gambled it away," Fargo criticized.

"I explained why," Toomey wearily said. "Equipment doesn't come cheap. Yes, it was a gamble, and yes, it was probably stupid of me, and if I had it to do over again, I wouldn't, but that's life." He studied Fargo intently. "Why all these questions? What do you care about my family?"

"I don't," Fargo said, and left. On the way out he passed the doctor, who snagged his sleeve.

"I thought you were watching my patient for me?"

"He's awake and gabbing up a storm," Fargo said, pulling free. "Tell him I'll be back to see him in the morning. Provided he is still alive."

"Where are you off to?" Dr. James inquired.

"To buy a bottle and see a lady and beat my head against a wall."

2

The brigantine was called the *Sea Hawk* and she was almost as old as Frank Toomey, but she was as seaworthy as any vessel in service. For days she had been forging steadily northward. The weather had cooperated and given them sun and not storm, and wind to fill the sails.

Fargo had not been on a ship in many months. He liked it. The constant roll of the deck did not make him sick as it did others, maybe because he was so used to the rolling gait of his pinto. He had left it stabled in Seattle. Better for the horse, he reasoned, than days cooped up in a dark pen belowdecks.

He loved to stand on the bow with the spray in his face and the wind in his hair. The bright glare made him squint, but it was no worse than the glare of the prairie on a hot summer's day, or the glare of a desert most any day of the year.

He was always on the lookout for sea creatures. Once he spotted whales, the great bulk of their enormous bodies rising up out of the sea with a grace that belied their size. Gray whales, the captain told him. They grew up to fifty feet long, and God knew how many tons.

"Devilfish, we call them," Captain Stevenson said.

"Why is that?" Fargo asked while admiring a behemoth that had reared up out of the deep.

"The females protect their young with the ferocity of

lionesses," Captain Stevenson related. "I have seen them kill orcas that tried to get at their calves. And once I saw a mother ram a boat that got too near her young one." The old salt had paused. "Strange, isn't it?"

"What?"

"That we call the young of whales and cows by the same name. Yet one lives in the sea and the other spends its days in a pasture."

The sixth day out, Fargo actually saw orcas. He was on the bow when several appeared to port, leaping clear of the water in flashing streaks of black and white.

The captain came up and grunted. "Grampus," he said sourly. "Killer whales. The wolves of the sea. They will attack and kill just about anything."

"You don't sound fond of them," Fargo noted.

"I'm not. I once saw orcas rip a baleen whale to near bits, then leave it helpless and in pain. They didn't eat it. They didn't finish it off. They just took delight in tearing it apart and swam merrily away." Stevenson spat over the side. "If you ask me, orcas are the true devilfish."

"Wolves eat what they kill."

"Eh? Oh. Rabid wolves, then. I have never heard of them killing a man but I would not care to be the one who puts them to the test."

The very next day Fargo spotted ten to twenty creatures that were black and white like killer whales but had much shorter dorsal fins.

As usual, Captain Stevenson was a fount of information. "Porpoises. They are often mistaken for orcas. You don't often see them this close to shore."

Suddenly one of the porpoises broke from the rest and sheered toward the brigantine. For a few moments, it looked as if the porpoise was going to slam into the bow, but instead it turned and rode the bow wave, keeping pace with the ship.

"They like to do that. Playful cusses," Captain Stevenson said. "The Japanese like to harpoon them and eat them, but that's not for me. I could never kill a porpoise or a dolphin. They're too friendly. Sometimes they almost act human."

That evening when it grew too dark to see much of anything except the blossoming stars, Fargo went belowdecks. He knocked on a particular compartment, and when he was bid to enter, did so.

Frank Toomey was propped in his bunk, reading a newspaper he had bought as they were about to board the *Sea Hawk* in Seattle.

"How are you feeling?" Fargo asked.

"Not bad," Toomey said with a smile. "I have most of my strength back, and my wrists don't hurt half as much."

There was no furniture. Fargo leaned against the bulkhead and folded his arms across his chest. "We'll be in Sitka by the end of the week."

"So the captain mentioned when he visited me earlier," Toomey said. "I suspect he thinks we are insane."

"I half think we are loco, too," Fargo said.

Toomey put down the newspaper. "Then why are you doing this? Why are you being so kind to me?"

"Who said I was?"

Frank Toomey swung his legs over the side of the bunk. "I don't know what to make of you. I truly don't. I lost my claim to you fair and square in that poker game. Yet you go and offer me half of it back without a word of explanation as to why."

Fargo shrugged.

"To me, that smacks of a good deed," Toomey said.

"Oh, hell. I'm as selfish as the next hombre." Fargo let out a sigh. "You say this mine of yours is a rich one, that there is a fortune just waiting to be dug out of the ground."

"There is!" Toomey said excitedly, waving his arms. "Just wait until you see the vein! Pure gold, as yellow as the sun!"

"Calm down or you will tear a suture."

"I can't help it," Toomey replied. "If you had seen it with your own eyes like I have, you would understand."

"Let's say you are right. Let's say there is a lot of gold to be had," Fargo allowed. "I'm no miner and I don't ever want to be. I don't know the first thing about running a mine. But you do."

"Ah. The light dawns. I do all the work, and you sit back and rake in your half of the profits without having to lift a finger."

"So much for my sainthood," Fargo said with a grin.

"Be honest with me," Toomey said. "You don't believe the strike is as rich as I have made it out to be, do you?"

Fargo was a while answering. "I would like for it to be true. I wouldn't mind having more money than I know what to do with. But gold fever is a common malady, and it wouldn't do for me to take your word for granted."

Toomey cocked his head. "If that is how you feel, then why in God's name did you offer to buy the equipment we need with your poker winnings?"

"You're forgetting something," Fargo said. "You don't get a cent until I have seen the claim with my own eyes. And once the mine is up and running, you are to pay back the money I lent you for equipment."

"You won't be disappointed. I promise," Toomey said.

Fargo bid him good night and went next door to his own compartment. He left the door ajar an inch or so to admit what little breeze wafted below deck. Lying on his back on his bunk with his fingers laced under his head, he stared up into the dark and said aloud, "Damn me for a fool."

The motion of the ship and the creak of the boards soon lulled Fargo into dozing off. He had always been a light sleeper and was even more so in the alien confines of the ship. He could not have been asleep long when suddenly his eyes were open again, and he lay listening for the sound he was sure must have awakened him.

A shoe scraped in the passageway.

Silently rising, Fargo cat-footed to the door and put his ear to the crack. Someone was whispering.

"We go in quiet and we go in quick and we do him

proper. Make sure you get a hand over his mouth so he can't cry out."

"How do we know he has the paper on him?" asked another. "Maybe he has it hid somewhere."

"I've told you. He always keeps it on him," said the first man, who had a nasal twang to his voice. "He has shown it to me often enough when I bring his food. It's all he ever talks about."

A third man chuckled. "Not much for brains, is the old landlubber?"

"He hasn't told me where the gold is, though," said the first, "so he's not completely dumb." He paused. "All of you have your blades ready? Good. Remember. Fast and quiet does it."

Fargo was already in motion. Bending, he slid his right hand under his pant leg and into his boot. Strapped to his ankle was an Arkansas toothpick. Not the large belt variety that rivaled bowies in size, but the original version, a short, slender, double-edged dose of wickedness.

Opening his door, Fargo slipped into the hall. He thought there were three of them but there were four. Crewmen he had seen nearly every day. Their ringleader was the cook, who had spent a lot of time with Toomey of late. Now Fargo knew why. The other three were typical of their breed—hardy, tough, and as salty as the sea. Their knives gleamed in the light of a lantern that hung on a peg at the end of the passageway.

The cook had opened Toomey's door and was peering inside.

Fargo glided up behind them. The last man either sensed or heard him and began to turn. Fargo did not tell him to drop his knife. He did not call on them to give up or shout for help. He simply stepped in close and buried his toothpick to the hilt in the seaman's back.

The would-be murderer bent like a bow and his mouth opened wide, but all he did was gasp. Then his eyes glazed and his legs buckled and he collapsed in a dead heap.

That gasp had been enough, though. The man in front

of him heard it, and whirled. With a sharp bark of anger, the man attacked, cleaving the air with a big knife.

Fargo sidestepped, slashed, and missed. The man crouched to come in low, his blade held close to his leg so Fargo could not see it. Fargo feinted to the left and the seaman took the bait and swung to parry the presumed strike. Which was exactly what Fargo wanted. For as the seaman swung left, Fargo went right, slicing the toothpick up and in between the man's ribs. Blood spurted from the man's nose and mouth and he collapsed against the bulkhead.

The third seaman had turned. A slab of muscle with an anvil for a chin, his knife was more like a cutlass. With a bestial growl he leaped, swinging his blade in an overhand stroke that would have split Fargo's head had it landed. But Fargo got the toothpick up in time. The clang of steel on steel was followed by the smack of Fargo's knees on the planking underfoot.

The big seaman whipped back his arm to swing again. In that brief interval, no more than the blink of an eye, his chest and throat were exposed. He hissed when the toothpick sheared into his jugular. Staggering back, he pressed a calloused hand to the wound but could not staunch the crimson flow. Sputtering and coughing, he keeled onto his side.

The cook was nowhere to be seen.

In a bound Fargo reached the doorway to Frank Toomey's compartment. From within came the sounds of a struggle. He burst in and beheld Toomey on his back on the floor with the cook above him. The cook had one knee on Toomey's chest and was striving to plunge his blade into Toomey's heart even as Toomey struggled with all his might to keep from being slain.

Fargo threw himself at the cook. But as swift as he was, he was not swift enough. The cook spun to confront him, wielding a butcher knife from the brigantine's galley.

"You!" The man glanced at the doorway. "Where are the other three?"

"They won't be slitting any more throats in the dead

of night," Fargo said, circling to get between Toomey and that butcher knife.

"We should have done you first," the cook said. "Up on deck where you would least expect."

"Give up," Fargo said.

"And be keelhauled? No, thanks. I'd rather it was over quick." And with that the cook attacked, swinging the butcher knife in a desperate frenzy.

Fargo had no choice but to give way. He parried, he dodged, he ducked, he skipped to either side, but he was forced inexorably back until he bumped into the bulkhead.

"Now I've got you!" the cook crowed, and lanced the butcher knife out and in.

Fargo twisted aside but not quite fast enough. A stinging sensation confirmed he had been cut. But he did not glance down. That would have been a fatal mistake, a mistake a greenhorn might make, and Fargo was no greenhorn—as the cook found out when Fargo opened his knife arm from wrist to elbow.

Howling in pain, the cook jumped back. He glared at the blood dripping from his arm, then at Fargo. "I'll gut you for that," he snarled, and switched the butcher knife from his right hand to his left.

"No, you won't."

They both looked toward the bunk. On it lay Frank Toomey's canvas bag, open. From the bag Toomey had taken a Dragoon Colt, an older model so large and cumbersome hardly anyone ever used them anymore. His hands shook as he thumbed back the hammer and pointed it at the cook. "Drop your knife. I won't tell you twice."

"Or what? You'll shoot me?" The cook snorted. "Maybe you didn't hear me tell your friend here that I'd rather die quick than slow. So go ahead. Blow out my wick."

"Please," Toomey said. "I've never shot anyone and I don't want to shoot you if I can help it."

"Is that a fact?" the cook taunted, and took a step toward him.

"Stop!" Toomey yelled, more of a bleat than a command. "I mean it! I will shoot if you force me."

The cook laughed and took another step.

"What were you after, anyhow?" Toomey tried to stall him. "What was this all about?"

"Can't you guess, you simpleton?"

"My gold mine? My claim? But it is filed under my name. The claim would do you no good."

"Only if I was caught before I dug out enough gold to last me the rest of my days," the cook said. He took a third step and drew back his left arm.

"Stop!" Toomey cried.

"Oh, hell," Fargo said. Drawing his Colt, he shot the cook in the head.

3

Sitka, Alaska.

Fargo learned a little of its history as the brigantine sailed north. The settlement got its start over sixty years earlier when a Russian trader by the name of Alexander Baranof decided that the site, on the west coast of a large island, was ideal for a trading post. With entrepreneurial flair he named the island after himself. A religious man, he named the settlement New Archangel.

Baranof chose well. Thanks largely to an abundance of lumber and fish, notably halibut and salmon, the settlement prospered and grew. It grew so fast that it was renamed the New World Paris. It also became the capital of Russia's Alaskan territory.

Later the name was changed to Sitka. The population was largely Russian, but there were many Americans and other nationalities, overseeing business interests.

Now, as the brigantine lowered her anchor and her sails, Fargo stood on the deck and surveyed the city he had sailed a thousand miles to reach. Most of the buildings were situated along a fertile belt between the sea and mountains that reared to the east. Snow crowned the highest peaks. To the north were cabins and homes, rustic and picturesque. The rest was the city proper, the government buildings painted white and constructed in the blockhouse style favored by Russian builders. The

Russian flag flew from a tall flagpole near a three-story building close to shore. Farther inland was a five- or six-story structure, the highest on the island.

"Sitka, at last," Frank Toomey said. "It won't be long now before we can head inland and you will see the claim for yourself."

Captain Stevenson came up. "A boat is putting out to meet us." He pointed at the dock. "Once they have boarded and inspected us, we will be permitted to go on shore."

"I can hardly wait," Toomey said eagerly.

Stevenson looked at Fargo. "I apologize, again, for the unpleasantness a few nights ago."

"You had nothing to do with it," Fargo said.

"No, I did not," the captain replied, with a pointed glance at Toomey. "Still, they were members of my crew, and I could be held accountable." He coughed and shifted his weight from one foot to the other. "Which is why I would like to ask a favor of you gentlemen."

"What kind of favor?" Toomey asked.

"That you say nothing of the incident to the Russian authorities. They can be sticklers about such things. They might take it into their heads to hold a formal inquiry, in which case I could be detained for months."

"But men died," Toomey said. "Surely we must report it?"

"To what end?" Captain Stevenson rejoined. "Will it bring them back from the seabed where we dropped them? We couldn't very well keep their bodies on board. By now the stench would have been frightful."

"I just meant—" Toomey began.

"If the Russians find out," Captain Stevenson cut him short, "it will create no end of problems for me and my crew. The Russians might even ban me from their waters. I would lose considerable income, no matter what they decide."

"You are asking a lot," Frank Toomey stubbornly maintained.

The captain focused on Fargo. "I appeal to you, then. You have been all over. You know how these things work.

Governments everywhere are the same. They delight in making us jump through hoops."

"We won't say anything," Fargo told him.

Frank Toomey put his hands on his hips. "I like that. You decide for the both of us? Is that how it goes?"

"If you want me to buy the equipment you need, yes," Fargo responded. "It's not the captain's fault those men tried to kill you. It's your own, for waving that claim around."

"I did not wave it," Toomey said resentfully. "I showed it to one person and one person alone. The cook. And I only showed it to him because he treated me so kind and considerate."

"I hope you are a better judge of gold than you are of men," Fargo said. "Whatever you do, from here on out don't show your claim to anyone unless you have to. And don't talk about it, either."

"Can I help it if I am proud of what I have done and want to brag a bit? I am only human."

"Finding a dollar in the street isn't a world-shaking accomplishment. It is luck."

"I see. You are implying I am too full of myself, is that it?"

Fargo sighed. "I am saying you better keep your damn mouth shut or someone else will do as the cook tried to do and slit your throat."

That gave Toomey pause. He stared at the approaching boat, then said, "Very well. It is against my better judgment but I will keep quiet."

"Thank you," Captain Stevenson said with great relief.

The boat contained an officer and six soldiers in addition to several civilians manning the oars. It came alongside the *Sea Hawk* and a ladder was lowered and the officer and the six soldiers came on board. All six wore bulky coats and hats and carried rifles.

The officer was a tall, striking man, his hair and mustache trimmed short, his bearing ramrod straight. He smiled warmly and offered his hand. "Captain Stevenson. It is a pleasure to see you again." His English was nearly flawless, with only a trace of an accent. "I take it you have brought one of your regular shipments and not special cargo."

"Captain Petrov," Stevenson said, shaking. "Just the usual supplies and a few passengers."

Petrov's dark eyes fixed on Fargo and Toomey. "So I see. Americans? On behalf of the Russian government I welcome you. Keep in mind that you are on Russian soil and under Russian law, and behave accordingly." He smiled and winked and lowered his voice so the soldiers would not hear. "And may I add, now that the formalities are out of the way, that you are free to do pretty much as you please, short of murdering someone, of course."

Frank Toomey looked down at the deck and frowned.

"Awful friendly of you," Fargo said.

"Not at all," Captain Petrov replied, and gestured grandly at the city that was known as the queen of the northland. "Soon all this will be yours, anyway."

"How's that again?" Fargo asked.

"Haven't you heard?" Captain Petrov said. "Your government has started talks with my government. America would like to buy Alaska from Russia."

Captain Stevenson said, "This is the first I have heard of it."

"Oh, yes," Captain Petrov declared. "Your Mr. Seward has made a few inquiries, and my government is interested."

"Your government would sell Alaska?" Frank Toomey asked in amazement. "*All* of it?"

"It is my fervent prayer, yes," Captain Petrov said.

"But there is so much land," Toomey persisted.

"Three hundred and sixty million acres, or so I have been told," Captain Petrov said. "I believe that is the equivalent of almost six hundred thousand square miles."

"Dear Lord," Toomey said in awe. "Why would Russia part with a paradise teeming with game and timber?"

"What does Alaska offer that Mother Russia does not have in abundance?" Captain Petrov rejoined. "Trees? We are thick with trees. Furs? We have many fur-bearing animals. Fish? Our rivers and the ocean are choked with fish." He shook his head. "No. Alaska had never been more than a colony to us. To give her up will be but a small affair."

"The American people will never go for it," Captain Stevenson said. "To most of them, Alaska is nothing but snow and ice and polar bears."

"Surely not," Captain Petrov said.

"Wait and see," Stevenson said. "The public will squawk to high heaven. Alaska is a long way from the rest of the States."

Fargo had little interest in their talk. Few things held less appeal to him than politics. He was more interested in the green hills and high mountains beyond Sitka, a wealth of land and wildlife rarely penetrated by white men. He would love to explore it some day.

Captain Petrov had turned to Frank Toomey. "We have met before, have we not?"

"I talked to you briefly before I left for Seattle," Toomey said.

"I remember now," Petrov said. "You have filed a claim with my government. For a gold mine, was it not?" He snickered, and caught himself.

"That amuses you?" Fargo said.

"I am sorry. But yes. Very little gold has been found in Alaska. That has not stopped men like Mr. Toomey, here, from wasting their lives searching for it. The hardships they endure, month after month of the most severe deprivation, and for what? A few grains of gold dust or, at the most, a few nuggets."

"There is more out there, I tell you," Frank Toomey declared. "More than anyone guesses."

"You know this how, Mr. Toomey?"

Toomey took his claim from a pocket and waved it in the air. "Because I have found a rich vein myself, and where there is one, there are more."

"For your sake I hope you are right," Captain Petrov said. "But for myself, I think you chase—what is it you Americans say? Oh, yes. A will-o'-the-wisp."

On that less than encouraging note, Fargo and Toomey climbed down into the boat and were taken ashore.

Toomey could not stand still, he was so excited. The instant they stepped onto dry ground, he snatched at the whangs on Fargo's sleeve and said, "Come on. I know a stable where we can rent horses. We will buy what grub and gear we need and be on our way at first light."

As much as Fargo wanted to see the claim site, he found himself saying, "Not so fast. We've been at sea for days. I want a hot meal and some whiskey. In the morning we will rent the horses and all the rest."

"But I thought—" Toomey said, and stopped, crestfallen. "I guess one more night won't hurt."

"Is there a hotel you recommend?" Fargo asked.

"Why spend money for a room when I have friends who will put us up for free?" Toomey started off up the street, beckoning for Fargo to follow. "You'll like Lester and Earl. They were up here looking for gold long before I showed up but they have yet to strike it rich."

Fargo was impressed by Sitka. It was not crowded and cramped like parts of New Orleans or St. Louis. The streets were broad, the buildings spaced well apart. There were trees and grass and even flowers.

The people had a robust vitality about them. The men of Russian extraction were big and brawny, the women big where women should be big. Heavy clothing was favored even though winter was months off yet. Everyone bustled about with a vigor lacking in cities far to the south.

They were passing a squat building with a high roof when the tinny refrain of a piano and a familiar odor brought Fargo to a halt. He regarded the sign that hung over the door. The Russian letters might as well be Greek. "Is this place what I think it is?"

Frank Toomey glanced at the sign. "You don't want to go in there."

"Answer the question."

"Yes, it is." Toomey said a word in Russian.

"A saloon?"

"The closest thing you will find anywhere in Sitka," Toomey confirmed. "But you really should not go in. You are asking for trouble if you do."

"Why?"

Toomey indicated the sign. "I can read and speak a little of the language. Enough to wrestle with a menu. This place is called the Motherland. Foreigners are not welcome."

"Is that a fact?" Fargo said, and walked in.

Frank Toomey did not follow him.

The place was crowded with Russians and only Russians. They were drinking, gambling, joking, laughing, doing all the things their American counterparts did for fun. It was no different from walking into a whiskey mill south of the Canadian border, except that in this instance everyone stopped talking and joking and laughing and the Motherland became as quiet as a tomb. A tense tomb, to judge by the stiff postures and the unfriendly stares cast in Fargo's direction. Ignoring them, cradling the Henry, he strolled to the bar.

A pair of burly patrons glared but moved aside. Fargo set the rifle down with a loud *thunk* and placed his bedroll beside it, then smacked the bar to get the bartender's attention. Not that he needed to. The bartender, like nearly everyone else, was giving him the sort of look that said he was distinctly unwelcome. "How about a drink?"

Scowling and wiping his thick fingers on his dirty apron, the stocky barkeep growled, "What you want, American?" His accent was atrocious.

"Didn't you hear me? I would like a whiskey and I would like it now." Fargo pounded the bar for emphasis.

A sly grin lit the bartender's unhandsome features. "No whiskey here. Only Russian drink. Only vodka."

"I'll take a vodka, then," Fargo said. He smiled at the men and women on either side of him but not one smiled back.

"You not like vodka," the bartender said. "Too strong. Too much for puny man. Go to Northern Lights. They have whiskey. Plenty whiskey."

Fargo pointed at a shelf behind the bar, a shelf lined with a variety of bottles. "No need. That's whiskey right there. Give me the bottle and a glass and you can go back to doing whatever it is you do when you're not lying to folks."

A red tinge crept from the bartender's thick neck to his nearly bald pate. "You mistake. That not whiskey. That vodka."

"Prove it," Fargo said. "Give me a taste."

The bartender leaned over the bar. "Leave, American. Leave or we make you leave."

"We?"

The bartender smirked and gestured.

Fargo slowly turned. Fully a third of the men were edging toward him. They had spread out in a half circle, cutting him off from the door. "So this is how it is."

4

The bartender was right. The smart thing for Fargo to do was get out of there while he still had all his teeth. Instead, he laughed at the menacing ring and said loudly, "Twenty against one? Is that your notion of fair odds? Where I come from, we call it yellow."

Several Russians started toward him but stopped at a word from another of their number seated at a table over against the wall. The man rose and kept on rising. He was a human bear, an impression heightened by his bushy black beard and mane of hair. A half-full glass in his hand, he came toward the bar. From the way others quickly moved aside, he was no ordinary reveler. He downed the contents of his glass as he approached and plunked it on the bar. "I am Vassily. I welcome you to Sitka."

"Someone with manners," Fargo said. "And your English is a lot better than Porky's."

"Porky, as you call him, is a friend of mine," Vassily said. "I do not take it kindly when my friends are insulted."

"I don't take kindly to insults, either. How about you let me buy you a drink and then you can buy me one?" Fargo proposed.

"It is not that simple," Vassily said.

"I didn't reckon it would be," Fargo said. "What do you have in mind?"

"I will try to beat you senseless. You will try to stop me from beating you senseless."

"And if I beat you senseless?"

Vassily's mouth quirked upward. "Many have tried but no one has ever done it. If you can, the drinks are on us."

"My kind of place," Fargo said, and hit him on the jaw. He did not hold back. He started his swing from below the hip and delivered an uppercut that should have stretched the Russian out on his back, unconscious. But the man called Vassily only staggered a few steps, and then, holding on to the bar for support, he slowly straightened and rubbed his jaw.

"Ready to give up?"

Vassily grinned and balled his fists. His knuckles were the size of walnuts. "On the contrary, American. I have never been hit as hard as you hit me. I am encouraged. You might be more of a challenge than I dared hope."

Fargo did not know where the fist came from. One instant the Russian was five feet away talking to him and the next instant a sledgehammer slammed into his jaw and he was knocked sprawling over a table. Shaking his head to clear it, he regarded Vassily with renewed interest. "Your punch has the kick of a mule."

"That is good, I take it. Although I spent two years at an American university in Boston, your figures of speech are sometimes confusing."

"It is a compliment," Fargo clarified.

"I begin to like you, American," Vassily said. "It is unfortunate I must teach you to show more respect for the customs of your hosts."

Fargo grinned wholeheartedly. "Me, I just need the exercise."

Vassily laughed and waded in, and for a while they battled toe-to-toe, trading blows and misses, each taking the measure of the other while trying to avoid being knocked out.

Fargo was no stranger to fistfights. He had been in more than a few, rarely by choice. He had learned a skill or three, and he put those skills to excellent use. He boxed as he had seldom ever had to. He blocked, he countered, he landed blows. He gave about as good as he got but he had to admit he was not faring as well as he expected. Vassily was good, very good, and plainly had his own share of fights under his wide leather belt.

They had been at it a solid five minutes, with the Russians hollering their heads off in support of Vassily, when the front door opened and in rushed a figure in uniform, trailed by Frank Toomey.

Vassily immediately stepped back and lowered his arms. Winking at Fargo, he whispered, "Be careful what you say, American." Then, adopting a broad smile, he spread his arms wide and declared in English, "Captain Petrov! What a pleasure to see you again. You so rarely come in here these days."

Petrov had a hand on the flap of his holster. "I have been informed a fight was taking place," he said suspiciously, "and when I came in, the two of you had your fists up."

"I was showing my American friend here the style of boxing we use in Mother Russia," Vassily said.

"And I am to believe that?" Captain Petrov demanded.

"Ask the American if you do not believe me."

The officer's dark eyes bored like twin drills into Fargo's. "Is he telling the truth? Were you having a friendly talk?"

"As friendly as this place gets," Fargo said.

Captain Petrov took his hand off his holster. "You do not do him a favor by protecting him. Vassily is a Baranof, a cousin of the man who founded this colony. But he is not here because he is an able trader or administrator. He is here because his own family has disowned him. In American parlance, Vassily is the black sheep of the Baranofs."

"Are you quite through?" Vassily asked.

The officer ignored him. "How you are associated with this man, I cannot begin to guess," he said to Fargo. "But I warn you. It is in your best interest to have nothing to do with him. He is not to be trusted. Not even a little bit."

Vassily had poured himself a drink. Taking a swig, he sighed with contentment, then said, "You must forgive the good captain. His manners are deplorable, but in his defense, he is only doing his job as he thinks it should be done. He and I have never seen eye to eye, you see. We are on what you would call the opposite sides of the fence."

"That we are," Captain Petrov agreed. "I am on the side of law and you are on the side of breaking the law."

"If that is true," Vassily replied, "why am I not in prison?"

"Because you are clever. That I will grant you. Clever enough that we can never tie you to the criminal activities you engage in."

"You have tried often enough," Vassily said.

"And I will go on trying until you are held responsible for your many crimes and spend the rest of your life behind bars." Captain Petrov smiled coldly at Fargo and departed, brushing Frank Toomey roughly aside.

"Is what he said true?" Fargo asked.

Vassily Baranof grinned. "I might have done a few things the law would frown on, but who among us has not? I do what I must to keep myself in vodka, good clothes, and women. No more, no less."

Frank Toomey picked that moment to tug at Fargo's sleeve. "Can we go? I want to get an early start tomorrow. It will take us over a week to reach my gold claim."

"Did he say gold?" Vassily asked.

"He found some fool's gold and thinks he is rich." Fargo tried to cover for them. Gripping Toomey by the elbow, he propelled him toward the entrance, saying in Toomey's ear, "You and that mouth of yours. Let's find those friends of yours and bed down for the night."

"What about your drink?"

"I made a mistake coming in here," Fargo said. He squinted as they stepped out into the bright glare of the sun.

"You admit it?"

"Yes, but not the mistake you think." Fargo steered the older man toward the corner of the building. He looked back but no one came after them.

"You sound mad at me. Did I do wrong going for help?" Toomey asked. "When I looked inside and saw they had surrounded you and were closing in, I thought they would hurt you. Then I saw Petrov heading for the government building and I ran to get him."

"It was kind of you." Fargo let it go at that.

On a hill overlooking the city stood a church, its architecture different from any church Fargo had ever seen. It reminded him of a painting in a restaurant in New Orleans of what the waiter said was a Gothic-style church in Europe. Atop it was a large stone cross.

On the other side of the hill, sprinkled among the trees, were cabins. Frank Toomey bent his steps to one of them and knocked on the door.

"Lester? Earl? It's me, Frank. Open up."

The door opened a crack and a bloodshot eye peered out. "It is you," the owner of the eye said, and opened the door all the way. The man who opened it had scraggly, dirty hair, and wore filthy clothes. His face was smeared with grime, and when he smiled at Toomey, he showed a mouth full of yellow teeth.

"Of course it's me," Toomey was saying. "What's gotten into you, Lester? You act like somebody is out to kill you."

"A man can never be too careful," Lester said. His brooding brows pinched together as he regarded Fargo. "Who's this? I don't know him."

Toomey introduced them, adding for Fargo's benefit, "Lester and his partner Earl were kind to me when I first came to Sitka. They took me in when I had nowhere to stay."

"That we did," Lester said. "And I can't say we are happy about the way you lit out of here without so much as a by-your-leave."

"I had to catch the ship," Toomey said.

"Where did you go? All we heard was you babbling about how you had made a strike and filed on it and were off to the States."

"I got as far as Seattle," Toomey said, and launched into an explanation of all that had happened to him since he left.

"So you think you have struck it big, huh?" Lester said, not without sarcasm.

"I know what you are thinking. That Earl and you have been up here for years and not found any gold to speak of yet, then I came along and found a rich vein in just a few months."

"Earl and me are old hands at prospecting," Lester said. "You're still green behind the ears."

"I've done it, I tell you," Toomey insisted. "And once the mine is up and running, I will repay Earl and you for your kindness. Wait and see if I don't."

"That's nice to hear," Lester said, but he did not sound all that grateful. Finally stepping aside, he bade them, "Come on in. You can have your usual cot, Frank. Your friend will have to sleep in the corner so he's not underfoot."

The cabin was as filthy as its owner. Used pots and pans and food-caked plates and bowls were piled on a counter. Blankets and clothes and tools and various other articles were scattered at random. The reek was almost enough to make Fargo gag. "I'll sleep outside."

"Suit yourself," Lester said. "But it gets mighty cold at night." He removed a pile of clothes from a cot. "Here you go, Frank."

A shadow filled the doorway. Instinctively, Fargo turned, leveling the Henry.

"Don't shoot me, pilgrim. I live here," said the unkempt apparition who ambled in. He had a moon face pockmarked with acne and a bulbous nose. Only slightly less filthy than his cabinmate, he held out a pudgy hand. "I'm Earl, by the way."

Fargo shook and was surprised at the strength in the man's grip. Again Toomey introduced him. He was surprised a second time when Earl threw his arms around Toomey and heartily clapped him on the back.

"It's grand to see you again, hoss! We were worried, what with you running off like you did."

"He thinks he's found the mother lode," Lester scoffed.

"Is that so? Well, it couldn't happen to a nicer fella. I am happy for you, Frank. I truly am."

Toomey turned to Fargo with a smile. "See? Didn't I tell you? A great couple of guys."

If you say so, was on the tip of Fargo's tongue, but he did not say it.

"I consider them two of the best friends I have," Toomey said. "I am glad I made their acquaintance."

"Is that so?" Lester said.

"I never lie. You know that," Toomey said. "When I say something is so, it is so."

Earl said to Lester, "You make an extra effort to be nice to Frank. I told you he thinks highly of us, didn't I?"

"I will be as nice as nice can be," Lester told him.

Fargo waited until supper was served—a greasy soup prepared by Earl—to bring up a few things he was curious about. "Why come all the way up here to hunt for gold when people say there's plenty yet to be had in the States?"

"I call that being nosy," Lester said.

"Now, now, Lester." Earl glanced at Toomey, laughed much too loudly, then said, "Well, it's like this, mister. Lester and me got into an argument with a gent over some mules. He insulted us and we insulted him and that made him so mad, he went for his gun. To keep from being shot we had to stick a knife in him."

"I did the sticking," Lester boasted.

Fargo found that interesting since neither Lester nor Earl wore revolvers or knives. But their clothes were baggy enough to hide an armory.

"The law didn't see it as we saw it," Earl went on, "and a warrant was issued for our arrest. Since we weren't partial to dangling from the end of ropes, we lit a shuck." He thumped the table with his knuckles. "This is where we ended up."

"Are there many more like you?"

"If by that you mean Americans, yes. I've never counted them but I'd say there are a couple of hundred. Traders, fur men, and the like."

"Many prospectors?"

"A few. It's not like California or Colorado where pocket hunters are as thick as fleas on a hound dog. But all it will take is one big strike and people will pour in from all over."

Fargo rose and carried his bedroll and the Henry to the door. "I'm fixing to turn in," he announced.

"See you in the morning," Toomey said. "If everything goes as it should, by noon we will be on our way. I can hardly wait."

Earl gave a little wave. "Sleep tight, you hear?"

"Give a yell if a wolf decides to nibble on you," Lester said.

Both men grinned.

5

The crunch of a heavy foot snapped Fargo out of a light sleep. He stayed perfectly still. He did not want whoever was stalking him to know he was awake.

Fargo had chosen a spot a stone's throw from the cabin to bed down. He had spread his blankets under a pine tree and sat down to wait. Before it grew dark he noted where every downed pine cone and twig within twenty feet lay. Once night descended, and those in the cabin could not see him, he had groped the ground, collecting as many of the pine cones and twigs as he could find. Then he had scattered them around his blankets, and was ready.

Now, in the pale starlight that filtered through the trees, a dark silhouette crept toward his blankets. In the silhouette's hand a blade glinted.

Fargo wondered which one it was: Lester or Earl. He drew his Colt but did not cock it. The man might hear.

With infinite patience the killer came closer. He was taking no chances, this one. He came to the blankets and raised his arm to stab.

Since Fargo did not care to have holes in his blankets, he stepped from behind the tree and thumbed back the Colt's hammer. "Looking for me?"

With a grunt of surprise, the man whirled.

"Drop the pigsticker and I might let you live," Fargo said.

The stalker did an incredible thing. He did not lower the knife. Snarling words in Russian, he attacked.

Fargo was almost taken off guard. The man was quick, ungodly quick, and the knife was spearing at his throat when his brain sent the impulse to his finger that caused it to tighten on the hair trigger of his revolver. The Colt boomed and bucked, and the figure was jolted but did not go down. Snarling more Russian, the man kept coming. Fargo shot him again, and yet a third time, and at the last blast the man pitched to his face in the dirt at Fargo's feet.

"Tough bastard," Fargo said.

Within moments there was a commotion in the cabin. The door opened and light spilled out. Toomey emerged, holding a lantern overhead. Lester and Earl were behind him, each with a rifle.

"What goes on here?" Toomey asked, running over. He saw the body and stopped cold. "My word, is he dead?"

"I hope so," Fargo said. He stared at Lester and Earl, then squatted and rolled the body over. The lifeless face the starlight bathed was that of a burly, bearded Russian. "I'll be damned."

"Who is he?" Toomey asked. "Why did you shoot him?"

Fargo held up the knife. "Our visitor wanted to stick this in me. Any idea who he is?"

"I've never set eyes on him before," Toomey said. "Or if I have, I don't remember. Russians tend to look alike to me."

"I've seen him before," Earl said. "He's one of that shadow bunch."

"The what?" Fargo asked.

"It's the best I can translate that gibberish they talk," Earl said. "It means those who live on the wrong side of the law." He hunkered and examined the dead man close up. "Yep. Definitely one. They don't rob banks or anything like that, but everything they do is shady. In the shadows." He began going through the man's pockets. "There are quite a few of this shadow crowd in Sitka. They had to leave the motherland for one reason or another and came here to get away."

"Like Lester and you," Fargo said.

Earl looked at him. "Yeah, like Lester and me." He slid his hand into another pocket and brought out a wad of Russian currency. "Look at this. Must be what he was paid to turn you into maggot food."

Frank Toomey nervously fidgeted. "What do we do with him? If Captain Petrov finds out, he will arrest Fargo."

"Who says Petrov has to find out?" Earl unfurled and listened, then chuckled. "No one is coming. If anyone heard, they probably figure it was a hunter shooting a deer or some such. We'll bury the body and no one will be the wiser."

"Except whoever sent him," Fargo said.

Toomey did more fidgeting. "I don't know. If the government finds out, we could be in a lot of trouble."

Earl spread his pudgy hands. "You can't have it both ways, Frank. Either we do what you think is right and report this and your new friend here is thrown behind bars or we keep our mouths shut and head out to your gold claim in the morning."

"What?" Fargo said.

Earl grinned from ear to ear. "Oh. That's right. You haven't heard. Frank wants Lester and me to go with you. Us being his pards and all."

A ferry took them to the mainland—a large flat-bottomed boat that could carry up to twenty people and half as many horses, operated by a surly Russian who accepted Fargo's money without comment and then did not say five words to them during the crossing. He put them off at an inlet, as instructed by Frank Toomey, and pushed off as soon as they and their animals were on shore.

"Friendly sort," Earl said.

"I hate all Russkis," Lester remarked. "They think

they are better than us but they don't wash any more often than we do."

For the first several days they paralleled the coastline, then struck off inland.

Wildlife was everywhere. The land teemed with creatures of all kinds, many of which showed little or no fear of man.

In the waters were ducks and geese. Osprey dived for fish or roosted in great nests high in trees. A variety of hawks, as well as bald and golden eagles, soared the air currents in search of prey.

Deer were as common as grass. There were plenty of elk, too. Every so often they spied moose, fortunately always at a distance, and the ungainly-seeming brutes would melt into the woods with no more sound than the whisper of the wind.

Black bears showed no fear of them. Twice they spotted grizzlies that showed no interest.

Smaller game was as abundant, if not more so. Squirrels chattered at them from tree branches, rabbits bounded off into the brush, and grouse took flight with a flurry of wings.

Fargo was in paradise. He had long loved the wild places. Wanderlust was in his blood, and there was nothing he liked more than venturing into country few if any whites had ever penetrated. From the Mississippi River to the Pacific Ocean, from the border with Canada to the border with Mexico, he had roved the frontier from end to end and back again, and he never tired of roving. Because for all he had seen, there was that much more he had not yet beheld. There was always something new over the next horizon.

Alaska was new. Alaska was virgin territory. Vast and largely unexplored, it was the last great frontier on the North American continent. Newspapers in the East portrayed it as an icy wasteland fit only for seals and polar bears, but nothing could be farther from the truth. Alaska was more akin to the Rocky Mountains than the Arctic. It had all a frontiersman could long for, and then some.

Fargo could be forgiven if he did not think much about

Toomey's claim, or how to deal with the complications that had sprung up. He was in heaven, and he could not get enough.

For five days after leaving the coast they forged steadily inland, into a rugged range with peaks that brushed the clouds. Some of the mountains were over three miles high. A couple, Fargo suspected, were closer to four. Many, according to Toomey, were capped with snow year-round.

The air was cool and crisp, the dank scent of the rich earth and the minty scent of the evergreens in Fargo's every breath. He became so absorbed in the spectacular scenery and the rich trove of wildlife that for once he failed to be as observant as he should, and it was Earl, not him, who announced in the middle of the morning on their sixth day in, "We are being followed."

Fargo drew rein and twisted in the saddle. Lower down and miles away, a line of riders was crossing a meadow.

"Indians, you reckon?" Lester wondered.

"Let's hope not," Earl said. "The Russkis have made so many enemies, most of the tribes hate all whites."

Toomey noticed Fargo's quizzical expression and said, "The Russians have not treated the Indians or the Eskimos very kindly."

Earl snorted. "Kindly, hell. The Russkis made slaves of a lot of them and wiped out any who objected. About fifty or sixty years ago, the Tlingits got so riled, they attacked Sitka. Massacred a heap of Russians and burned Sitka to the ground."

Toomey nodded. "The Russians rebuilt Sitka and exterminated as many of the Tlingits as they could catch."

"So let's hope it's not Tlingits," Earl said. "Them and the Aleuts don't mind killing whites one little bit."

Fargo was studying the line of riders. They were too far off to tell if they were white or red, but not too far off to count. "I make it close to twenty."

"Hell," Earl said.

"And they are smack on our trail."

Earl shifted for another look. "Double hell. I don't believe in coincidence. They must be following us."

"Maybe not," Frank Toomey said. "Maybe they are hunters, or a party of prospectors, or it could be a government patrol."

"You always look at the bright side, don't you?" Earl scoffed. "Hunting parties usually have five or six men at the most. Prospectors tend to be solitaries. And the Russians hardly ever send patrols this deep in unless they have a damn good reason."

"What are you suggesting?" Toomey asked.

"I'm not *suggesting* anything," Earl replied. "I'm saying we had better be on our guard from here on out."

Fargo agreed. He had his own notion about the mystery men but he kept it to himself for the time being.

Soon they were in heavy timber, and they stayed in heavy timber for the rest of that day and most of the next. Toward evening they came out on a largely barren slope strewn with boulders. A small stream offered water, and they decided to stop for the night next to it.

By mutual consent they had agreed to take turns with the camp chores. One night Fargo would cook while Earl and Lester stripped the horses and Toomey foraged for kindling and fuel. The next night Earl might cook while Fargo searched for firewood and Toomey and Lester attended to the animals. On this particular night, Fargo and Toomey were unsaddling the animals when Toomey cleared his throat and said, "I'm worried."

"About time," Fargo said.

"Why do you say that? What do you know that I don't?"

Fargo undid the bay's cinch. "I know you are too trusting, and I know you can't keep your mouth shut. Put those two together and you should have been worried before we left Sitka."

"That's unkind and untrue," Toomey said resentfully. "It's not as if I erected a sign telling everyone I found gold."

"You might as well have," Fargo said.

Earl cooked supper. They had venison left from a buck Lester shot two days previous, and Earl placed strips of the deer meat in a frying pan and put the pan on a flat rock next to the flames. Soon the crackle and sizzle had their mouths watering. Earl also made dodgers and brewed coffee.

Fargo was famished. He ate two dodgers smeared with butter and was chewing a slice of deer meat when Lester asked a question that was on his own mind.

"How much farther to the gold, Frank?"

Toomey regarded the nearby peaks and scratched the stubble on his chin. "Another three days, maybe."

But three more days went by and it was obvious to the rest of them that Frank Toomey was lost. He took to muttering to himself and gazing perplexedly at the surrounding peaks.

At noon the next day, they stopped to rest the horses. Fargo walked over to the log on which Toomey rested and came right out with it, "You don't have any damn idea where we are, do you?"

Toomey reacted as if he had been stabbed. "I can't understand it. I was sure as sure can be that I was following the same route. But there's been no sign of the next landmark."

"What would that be?" Fargo asked.

Earl and Lester were listening with keen interest.

"I guess there is no harm in sharing," Toomey said, and once again gazed at the mountains they were wending through. "The next landmark is a peak. A barren rock peak split down the middle. We should have seen it two days ago."

"I have an idea," Fargo said. He pointed at a heavily timbered mountain half a mile off to the northwest. "We climb that one clear to the top. From up there we should be able to spot your rock peak if it is anywhere within fifty miles."

Once their animals were rested, they struck out for the mountain. By nightfall they were a third of the way up. The slopes were steep, the going arduous. There was talus to avoid and deadfalls to skirt. Evening found them on a broad bench that overlooked their back trail, and they had barely settled in when Earl gave a holler.

Fargo ran with the others to where Earl stood at the

edge of the bench. Miles below were several reddish-orange fingers of flame.

"Campfires," Toomey said. "They are still back there, and taking their sweet time."

"They want the gold," Fargo said. "They won't close in until we reach your claim."

Earl laughed. "That could be a good long spell. It will serve them right if we don't find it. Another week or two of this and them and their animals will be tuckered out."

"And us and ours," Fargo said.

They went back to their own fire. It was Lester's turn to cook. Earlier Fargo had dropped three grouse on the wing, and Lester busied himself chopping off the heads and legs and plucking the feathers. He had been at it a while, and the ground was littered with feathers and spattered with blood, when their horses suddenly raised their heads and pricked their ears and whinnied.

"Something is out there," Toomey said.

Taking a brand from the fire, Fargo snatched up his Henry and moved to a point between the horses and the timber. He raised the torch aloft but saw only a shadowy wall of vegetation.

The thing off in the dark uttered a low, rumbling growl.

"Oh, hell," Earl said. "It's a bear."

Fear tinged his tone, and Fargo did not blame him. Few creatures anywhere were as formidable as bears, particularly grizzlies. He levered a round into the Henry's chamber.

"Don't shoot unless it shows itself, and if you do shoot, shoot to kill," Earl said. "A wounded bear is next to unstoppable."

Fargo was well aware of that. He wedged the Henry to his shoulder. "If it goes after the horses I will try to hold it off while you get them out of here."

"Better you than me," Earl said with a forced grin.

"What kind do you think it is?" Toomey asked. "A black bear or a griz?"

"Neither," Fargo said, and used his rifle to point into the woods.

Frank Toomey gasped.

At the fringe of the light cast by their torches, and some ten to twelve feet off the ground, glowed a pair of eyes.

Only one creature in all of Alaska was that big.

6

"Dear God in heaven!" Earl whispered. "It's a brown bear!"

Fargo had encountered bears many times. Black bears were common west of the Mississippi, and usually fled at the sight of humans. Grizzlies thrived in the Rockies, although there were not as many as in the days of Lewis and Clark. Grizzlies were more aggressive, but nine times out of ten, a grizzly, too, would lope off when it encountered a human, content to mind its own business.

Black bears and grizzlies. The two most common kinds of bear found in North America. But they were not the *only* kind.

Much farther to the north, where the ice ruled and winter reigned nine months of the year, polar bears were the undisputed lords of all they surveyed, feasting on seals or walrus or whatever else was hapless enough to succumb to their slashing claws and razor teeth—people included. Polar bears were notorious for their savage temperament. To a polar bear, everything else, human beings included, was flesh waiting to be eaten.

Polar bears, even more than grizzlies, were universally feared. But there was one bear feared even more. One bear that filled Eskimo and Indian and white man alike with fear so potent, it paralyzed the limbs and turned minds to mush.

That bear was the Alaskan brown bear.

Its ferocity was legendary. On the voyage from Seattle, the brigantine's skipper had related tales of brown bear attacks that would curl the hair. It was not their carnivorous natures alone, for polar bears and grizzlies were just as fierce. What made brown bears even more formidable, and more widely dreaded, was their sheer size.

Brown bears were some of the largest bears and some of the largest meat eaters anywhere in the world, far larger than lions and tigers and twice as heavy as their Ursine kin, the grizzly. The brown bears of Kodiak Island and other parts of Alaska were especially noted for their immense bulk. A full-grown male could be over ten feet long and weigh upwards of fifteen hundred pounds. Nothing could stand up to them. They went where they wanted and did as they pleased and woe to any puny humans who got in their way.

And here was Fargo, not twenty feet from one of the monsters, its shaggy head looming gigantic in the night, its feral eyes blazing like the orbs of a demon spawned from a nether realm.

"Shoot it!" Frank Toomey bleated, and brought up his rifle to fire.

"No!" Fargo swatted the barrel down.

Toomey took a step back in surprise. "What are you doing?" Again he went to raise his rifle, and this time it was Earl who grabbed the barrel and wrenched the weapon from his grasp.

"Use your head, Frank! All you'll do is make it mad, and the last thing we want is to rile it."

"But the horses!" Toomey protested, snatching at his rifle.

Earl jerked it away. "Quiet down! Or so help me, I will bean you with your own gun."

The brown bear picked that moment to give voice to a roar that sent the horses into a panic. Lester and Earl dashed over to calm them. Toomey was rooted in shock.

Fargo stood rooted as well, but not for the same reason. Someone had to cover them. He kept the Henry's sights on that enormous triangle of hair and bone and teeth, hoping against hope the bear would not charge. He was under no illusions about the outcome. A bear's skull was incredibly thick and proof against all but the heaviest caliber firearm. A brown bear's skull was the thickest of all, and dropping one was like trying to drop a steam locomotive.

"I've never seen any up close like this," Toomey said. "I never realized how big they are." He started to back away.

"Stand still!" Fargo snapped, but not too loudly.

"The others moved. They ran to the horses," Toomey complained.

"We were lucky," Fargo said. Lucky that it had not provoked the brown bear into attacking. One of the first lessons he had learned when he came west was to never, ever flee from a meat eater. "Or as sure sure as shootin'," said the old-timer who had imparted the wisdom, "they will come after you."

The Indian tribes Fargo had lived with agreed. To flee from a bear or a mountain lion or a wolf was to invite them to chase you, and all three could run faster than any human who ever lived. Fargo had taken the advice to heart, and on more than one occasion it had saved his hide.

The brown bear took a lumbering step toward them. Erect on its hind legs, it resembled a beast out of antiquity, the kind the newspapers loved to write about whenever prehistoric bones were found.

"Oh God," Toomey said. He was poised to bolt.

"If you run I will shoot you," Fargo threatened. And he would, too. In the leg or the arm.

The brown bear took another shuffling step, and now they could see its huge forepaws and the long claws that could shear through flesh and bone as a bowie sheared through paper.

Toomey would not shut up. "Oh God, oh God, oh God, oh God."

"Don't talk," Fargo commanded.

"Why not? What can it hurt? It's not like the bear will attack us just because I'm talking."

The man would never know how close he came to having his head introduced to a rifle stock. Fargo was tensing to slam the Henry against the side of Toomey's head when the brown bear abruptly dropped onto all fours and came toward them.

"We're doomed!" Toomey shrieked, and fled toward the fire.

Fargo did not move. He fixed a bead on the monster's right eye as the eye grew steadily larger. Suddenly the brown bear was in front of him, its black twitching nose inches from the Henry's muzzle. The wheeze of its lungs was like the wheeze of a bellows. Fargo swore he could feel its warm, fetid breath fan his cheeks. He could see every hair, see its nostrils flare, see into the depths of its bottomless eyes. His skin prickled, and he braced for an onslaught of fang and claw.

Then the miracle occurred. Or maybe it was not a miracle. Maybe it was the bedlam, the whinnies and the shouts and the squalling of Toomey for someone to shoot the thing. Bears did not like loud noise. So maybe that was why the brown bear unexpectedly turned and crashed off into the brush.

Fargo did not lower the Henry until the sounds faded. Letting out the breath he had not known he was holding, he walked to the fire, set down the Henry, and poured a cup of coffee.

Toomey was beaming. "It didn't attack us!"

"No thanks to you." Fargo hunkered and took a sip, and it was just about the most delicious coffee he ever tasted.

"I'm sorry. I was scared. I couldn't help myself."

Fargo's disgust knew no bounds but he bit off a sharp retort. "How did you ever make it in and out the last time?"

"I'm not totally helpless," Toomey said.

"You could have fooled me, Frank." This from Earl, who followed Fargo's example. With his battered tin cup in his hands, he sank down cross-legged. He sipped and smacked his lips.

The horses had quieted down now that the brown bear

was gone. Lester was checking that none of the picket pins had been pulled loose.

"I have had some close shaves in my day," Earl commented, "but that was one I could have done without."

"It might take it into its head to come back," Fargo said. "We should stand guard tonight. I'll take the first watch."

Presently Earl and Lester turned in, and Lester was soon snoring loud enough to be heard in Sitka.

Frank Toomey nursed a cup of coffee until the coffee had to be cold. He glanced at Fargo several times as if about to speak.

"If you have something on your mind, say it," Fargo finally prompted.

"I don't want you to think poorly of me."

Fargo looked at him. He wondered if Toomey realized he already did. "Care to explain?"

"I did find gold. I bet my claim knowing I might lose, and I had no hard feelings when I did." Toomey grinned. "Well, almost none."

"Understood," Fargo said.

"There's more. You see, Earl's comments have me worried you might think I am trying to trick you. That I know where the gold is but I am misleading you so you will give up and go back to the States and I will have all the gold for my own."

Fargo waited.

"That is not the case. I have been sincere with you from the beginning. I am a man of my word."

"If I thought you weren't, I wouldn't be sitting here," Fargo said.

"Thanks. I just wanted you to know. I am trying my best. But I am not a scout, like you. My sense of direction leaves a lot to be desired. As for how I made it in and out the last time, I will tell you a secret I have not told anyone, not even Earl and Lester." Toomey paused. "I had a guide."

"You what?"

"An old Indian. He came up to me out of the blue and said he had heard I was looking for the yellow metal and would I like for him to show me some. Naturally, I said yes. He brought me right to the spot and took me out again."

"This old Indian have a name?"

"He had an Indian name I couldn't pronounce so he had me call him Gray Fox. He said that was what all the whites call him. On account of his gray hair, I guess."

"What tribe was he from?"

"I didn't ask and he didn't say and I can't tell one from the other," Toomey replied, and sighed. "I wish Gray Fox was here now. He could lead us to the gold with no problem."

Fargo had one more question. "What did he get out of it?"

"Pardon?"

"What did he want in return for taking you to the gold?" Fargo clarified. "I doubt he did it out of the goodness of his heart. Not when so many of the tribes in these parts hate whites."

Toomey was stunned. "I never gave that any thought. But you know, now that you mention it, he never did ask for anything in return, not so much as a dollar. That's a bit peculiar, wouldn't you say?"

"I would say it was a lot peculiar," Fargo amended. And troubling. Yet another complication he could do without.

Toomey set down his coffee cup and stood. "Well, I just wanted you to know where I stood so you would not think poorly of me."

"You shouldn't be here," Fargo came right out and said it.

"Excuse me? I have a half-interest in the claim. You gave it back to me, remember?"

"By here I meant *here*." Fargo gestured to encompass their wild surroundings. "You should not be in Alaska. You should not be anywhere on the frontier. You should be in a rocking chair in front of a hearth in a cozy house somewhere east of the Mississippi. Somewhere where it is safe to walk the streets at night."

"I am out of my element—is that it?"

Fargo did not say anything.

"I appreciate the sentiment. I truly do. And since we are being honest with one another, I will admit you have a point. I am no woodsman. I was raised in a city, not the country. But I had to do this. I just had to."

"No one ever has to do anything if they do not want to," Fargo said.

"I want to." Toomey hesitated, then sat back down. "I want to amount to something. I want money, lots and lots and lots of money, even if I leave most of it to my children and my grandchildren. That is why I came to Alaska in the first place. For their future, not for mine."

"But the odds—" Fargo began.

"I know, I know. For every ore hound who strikes it rich, a thousand end up with empty bellies. But I did not let that stop me. I felt in my bones that it was my destiny, that the Almighty was on my side, if you will." Toomey was growing excited. "And I was right! It was a miracle, that old Indian coming to me. It was a miracle, him leading me to gold. Now I *will* amount to something. Now my family will look up to me. All my prayers will come true."

"When something is too good to be true," Fargo said.

"It probably is," Toomey finished. "Yes, I have heard the saying. But in this instance, it does not apply. I have seen the gold with my own eyes. It is there. It is real." He stood again. "I will prove it to you. I will show you that your trust in me is not misplaced. Wait and see if I don't." With a smile and a nod he moved toward his blankets.

Fargo refilled his cup and sat back. He sipped and pondered and listened to the chorus of bestial cries that filled the Alaskan night: the howls of wolves; the snarls and grunts and occasional roars of bears; the ear-piercing shrieks of mountain lions; the screeches of the lesser cats; the hooting of owls; and the bleat of prey taken by predators. It was a riotous din of primal life in all its many savage facets.

Fargo loved it. That many of the creatures he was hearing would devour him if they could was incidental.

The wilds had the same pull on him that gold had on men like Frank Toomey. He could never get enough, no matter how far or how long he wandered.

He reminded himself to never lose sight of the fact that for all its breathtaking beauty and natural splendor, the wild places were dangerous places. A single misstep could get a man killed. Sometimes a man did everything right and still became worm food. It was simply how things were.

A snore from Lester drew Fargo's gaze to the sleepers. They had made it this far, but as Earl had noted, there was no guarantee any of them would survive to see Sitka again.

Forces other than the land and the animals were conspiring against them. As if that were not bad enough, some of his own party could not be trusted.

Off in the brush, there was a flurry of sound and movement. A bird was pounced on and twittered its death cry.

"Hell of a note," Skye Fargo said.

7

At first light they were up. By sunrise they had resumed the climb. It was slow, laborious going, with some of the slopes too steep or too treacherous for the horses.

Frank Toomey was in excellent spirits. He hummed and whistled and beamed at the world until Earl said, "Will you *please* quiet down? I am a grump in the morning and you are not helping my disposition any."

By ten they reached timberline. Hardly had they emerged from the trees than Frank Toomey twisted back and forth in his saddle, threw out an arm, and exclaimed, "There! There! What did I tell you? Do you see? Exactly as I said it would be."

That it was. A stark, barren, rock peak, split by some cataclysm of yore, perhaps ten miles to the northwest as the raven would fly.

"We won't get there until late tomorrow," Lester said. "How much more after that to the gold?"

"Another day, possibly two."

Fargo had been keeping an eye on their back trail. Now reining around, he surveyed the expanse of wilderness below and said, "No sign of whoever is following us."

"They don't know that we know they are dogging us, and they will want to keep it that way," Earl remarked.

They worked their way around to the other side of the

mountain and descended. Once they flushed a bevy of grouse. Later several elk disappeared into the pines, amazingly silent for animals so large. Later still an eagle winged overhead, so near that they heard the beat of its wings and saw it cock its head and study them.

By pushing hard, they were within two miles of the stony peak when the sun perched on the western horizon. Earl shot a doe, which he and Lester butchered, and that evening they dined on succulent venison and beans. Fargo did the honors. Everyone ate their fill and turned in early.

Morning came, and Earl and Lester were almost as excited as Toomey. They threw on their saddles and headed out, leaving Fargo to lead the pack animal. Since he was taking his time and paying attention to what went on around them, he was the one who spotted tendrils of smoke to the west and shouted to get the attention of the others.

"Who the hell can that be?" Earl wondered aloud. "The ones who are following us are to the south."

"It could be anyone," Toomey said. "Hunters, fellow prospectors, anyone."

"Just so they don't show up at the claim," Lester said, "or word will get back to Sitka and we will be in gold-crazed yacks up to our ears."

That night they camped at the base of the stone peak. As soon as the sun was up they were under way, Toomey practically giddy with glee. "Do you see this stream?" he asked when they came on a gurgling blue ribbon. "It is the most important landmark of all. I can't possibly get lost now."

All they had to do was stick with the stream, he informed them, to where it flowed out of a long, winding valley, lush with grass. Lo and behold, they soon came to a valley, and rode up into it.

Toomey giggled with glee. "We are so close I can barely sit still!"

A quarter of a mile in, they abruptly drew rein. Their way was barred by a herd of animals unlike any Fargo ever set eyes on. In size and shape they reminded him of buffalo. The males stood five feet high at the shoulders, whereas male buffalo stood six. In length they were slightly smaller, too, the males being about eight feet long, as opposed to twelve feet for a mature buffalo bull. They had broad heads, like buffalo, and dark, shaggy hair that was much longer, hanging down to the ground on some of the males. Both sexes had horns. Those on the females were short and curved. Those on the males had a spread of two and a half feet and were thicker than those of buffalo. They had big eyes, thin lips, and pointed ears.

"Musk ox," Earl declared.

The brutes were aptly named. Fargo caught a whiff of a strong odor. Urine, unless he was mistaken.

"We better be careful and swing wide," Earl advised. "They can be as cantankerous as moose."

There were over thirty in the herd. At a bellow from a male, the older males and females formed a protective ring around the younger ones, presenting a phalanx of horns.

"I saw a wolf try to break through a line of musk ox to get at a calf once," Earl related. "They gored it and tossed it into the air, then trampled it to a pulp. Gave me a whole new respect for anything with horns."

Both the males and females were snorting and stomping the ground, and some of the larger males were bellowing their challenge. Suddenly a male broke from the ring and came toward them with its head held low.

"Damn!" Earl said, and brought up his rifle.

But the musk ox came only halfway, then wheeled and rejoined the line. A second bull imitated the first and again went back without attacking.

"They are trying to scare us off," Toomey said.

"And doing a good job of it." Earl grinned. "I'd rather tangle with that brown bear we ran into than these critters."

Not Fargo. Bears were the most unpredictable creatures on earth, and the most formidable. Grizzlies were especially hard to kill. He had heard of a mountain man reputed to have slain close to thirty, but he figured that was whiskey talk. No one could run into that many and live to tell of it.

Reining to the left, they gave the angry musk ox a wide berth. Once they were past, the herd quieted and resumed feeding.

"You never know what you are going to run into out here," Earl remarked. "If it ain't chickens, it's feathers."

"So long as we don't run into hostiles," Lester said. "They spook me some. It's the carving they do. I'd rather be buried with all my parts than shy a few."

"When I go I hope it is quick," Earl said. "In bed would be nice. Maybe while I am diddling a dove."

"What a thing to talk about," Toomey said. "Dying."

"We all do, sooner or later," Earl replied. "Might as well accept it so when the time comes you don't scream and bawl."

"You are a bundle of surprises, Mr. Marsten."

Only then did it hit Fargo that he had not known Earl's and Lester's last names. Not that it mattered. As Earl had just pointed out, dead was dead.

The valley wound on, mile after mile, becoming more wooded. They were rounding a bend when something snorted and came crashing out of the undergrowth.

Instantly, they drew rein. Fargo was in the lead, Toomey and Earl behind him, Lester at the rear with the packhorse. "No one move," Fargo said. He had his hand on his Colt but he doubted it would drop the engine of sinew and horn that confronted them.

It was a moose. A male moose, notoriously belligerent, and with the might to hold its own against any comer. This one stood almost eight feet at the shoulder and had to weigh close to three-quarters of a ton. Its antlers put those of a musk ox and a buffalo to shame. Five feet from tip to tip, they were broad and flat and could fling a wolf, or a man, through the air with a mere flick. A dewlap hung from under its chin.

Fargo waited for the moose to make up its mind whether it was going to attack. Reining around and riding off would do no good. Moose could run as fast as horses. They had been known to charge people without provocation. Males in rut would charge anything; one reportedly charged a steam locomotive once.

"Why don't you shoot it?" Toomey whispered.

"No," Fargo said.

Earl gigged his horse forward, saying, "Hell, if you won't, I will. Moose jerky is as tasty as any other, and there's enough meat on this one to last us a month of Sundays."

"Stay still," Fargo urged, but the harm had been done.

With an angry bellow, the moose lowered its head and charged. Earl was bringing up his rifle but he did not quite have it level when the moose slammed into his horse. Horse and rider spilled in a tangle of limbs and the moose went running on past.

Fargo hoped it would keep on running. It was doing just that when Lester's rifle banged, and instantly the moose wheeled and charged again, this time hurtling toward Frank Toomey.

"Help me!" Toomey squawked, slapping his legs against his mount in a frantic bid to escape.

Lester's rifle boomed again as Fargo yanked the Henry from his saddle scabbard. He worked the lever, injecting a round into the chamber, but before he could aim and fire, the moose rammed Toomey's horse and both crashed down, the horse squealing in fright.

Earl had scrambled to his feet. He had lost his rifle when he went down and was casting wildly about for it.

"Shoot it!" Lester bawled at Fargo. "What in hell are you waiting for?"

Fargo wanted to be sure. He had the Henry to his shoulder as the moose spun with surprising agility and bore down on them yet again. This time it was barreling toward the bay, its antlers held low to rip and disembowel. He fired at its head, banging off two swift shots.

At the second blast the moose veered aside. But it did not run off. It charged Lester and the packhorse.

Crying out in alarm, Lester hauled on his reins and tugged on the lead rope. Neither prevented the moose from slamming into the pack animal and upending it where it stood. The lead rope was wrenched from Lester's grasp, nearly spilling him from the saddle.

The moose tripped and almost went down but recovered and spun once more. Its long head swung toward Fargo and the antlers lowered for the spurt of speed that would precede impact.

Fargo squeezed the trigger, jerked the lever, squeezed the trigger again. The moose was forty feet out and he fired once more, thirty feet and he fired, and then twenty feet and Fargo sent yet another slug into its brow. He braced for the jarring jolt of its heavy form and slid his boots free of his stirrups so he could spring clear at the last instant, but that instant never came.

Its forelegs buckling, the moose crumpled. Momentum carried it to a sliding stop an arm's length from the bay.

Fargo aimed at the head but he did not shoot. Instead, he lowered the Henry. Another shot was unnecessary.

The eyes of the moose were open but glazing and its tongue was lolling out.

Earl, lustily swearing, had recovered his rifle. Lester was worriedly examining the packhorse.

Toomey was still on the ground, flat on his back with an arm over his face. "Is it safe?" he asked.

"You can get up," Fargo said.

Toomey gazed fearfully about. When he saw the moose he smiled and slowly rose to his knees. "I thought I was done for. That was the scariest thing that ever happened to me."

"Aren't you forgetting the men who tried to kill you on the ship?" Fargo reminded him.

"The cook wasn't as big as this moose," Toomey said.

Both his mount and Earl's were back up and unharmed except for a gash on the buttermilk's flank. The packhorse, though, was still down, and would stay down this side of the grave. Its belly had been opened and its insides were oozing out in a spreading pool of organs and gore. Weakly thrashing its legs, it tried to stand but lacked the strength.

"Damn, damn, damn," Earl fumed. "We don't have a

horse to spare, and this has to happen." In his fury he stepped over to the moose and kicked it.

Some of the packs had been knocked loose, their contents spilled. Lester started to gather them up, heaping muttered oaths on all moose in general and the dead moose in particular.

Toomey was staring sadly down at the pack animal. "One of us should put this poor thing out of its misery."

"You have a rifle," Earl said.

"I'd rather it was someone else," Toomey told him. "I have always been squeamish when it comes to killing."

"It's a horse, not a person, for God's sake."

"I'm sorry. I was never much of a hunter." Toomey turned away. "Please. Can't one of you do it?"

Fargo had listened to as much as he could abide. The horse was suffering, suffering greatly. It might be hours before it succumbed. He touched the Henry's muzzle to its head.

"Thank you," Toomey said gratefully.

Earl shook his head. "Don't get mad at me for saying this, Frank, but you are next to worthless sometimes."

"I do what I can," Toomey said.

"What I want to know," Lester said, "is what we are going to do about these packs. I would hate to have to leave the flour and sugar and the rest of our food to spoil or be eaten by varmints."

They talked it over and decided to divide the packs equally among them. Each man then tied those he was responsible for onto his horse. Within half an hour they were on the move again.

A lightning-charred spruce was cause for Toomey to rise in the stirrups and exclaim, "See that? We are almost there! Ten minutes at the most."

"That soon?" Lester said. He looked at Earl, who shook his head. Both glanced at Toomey to see if he had noticed.

Fargo had. He was riding with the Henry across his thighs, his thumb on the hammer, his finger on the trigger. "How easy is it to spot?" he asked.

"You have to know where to look," Toomey said. "It's

why I have not been too worried about someone robbing me of what is rightfully mine." He caught himself. "Rightfully ours, I mean, since you have as much at stake as I do."

Another bend brought them to the valley's end. Slopes rose on either side to a peak high above.

"What the hell?" Earl said, turning this way and that. "Where is this vein you keep bragging about?"

Fargo looked, too. He was no prospector but it was plain as plain could be. There was nothing there.

8

"O, ye of little faith," Frank Toomey quoted, and gigged his horse to a stand of aspens. Dismounting, he beckoned.

Fargo swung down. He cradled the Henry and followed Toomey into the stand. Earl and Lester were behind him.

"I never did ask Gray Fox how he found the gold," Toomey was saying. "But he did mention he has been all over these mountains. As old as he was, I believe him."

The stand was small. Thirty feet from where they entered it the aspens ended yards from a rock cliff not much higher than the aspens themselves and not much wider than a log cabin. The rock was laced with quartz. Not a lot, but enough to be promising. Gold was often found with quartz.

"Where is it?" Lester impatiently demanded.

"Hold your horses," Toomey said, and sank to his knees at the base of the rock cliff. He began scraping at the dirt.

"Don't you want a shovel?" Earl asked.

"I don't need one," Toomey said while continuing to scrape. "It's not solid earth."

An inch down was a lattice of interwoven aspen branches. Roughly circular and about the size of a large basket, it had been fashioned with gaps so fingers could be inserted and the whole thing lifted like a lid. As he gripped it, Toomey said, "This was Gray Fox's idea. He made it for me. Indians can do clever things with their hands."

The lattice covered a hole. In the shadow of the cliff it looked deeper than it was, as Fargo found when he stepped to the edge. Two feet deep was all, enough to expose a yellow vein. He could no longer doubt. Not when the evidence was before his eyes.

"There it is," Toomey said, beaming.

"Gold!" Lester breathed.

Earl squatted, braced a hand on the edge, and slowly reached down to touch the precious ore. "I'll be damned. You did it. You really did it."

"I told you," Toomey said.

"Yes, you did, Frank, and I am sorry I did not entirely believe you," Earl said, running his hand along the vein almost as if caressing it. "It is human nature, I reckon."

"I suppose," Toomey said, and glanced at the sky. "Do we start digging now or wait? The sun will set in less than an hour."

"We should dig now," Lester said.

"No," Earl responded. "We have been in the saddle all day, and we're tired. The gold isn't going anywhere. I say we rest up and start in the morning. We'll be fresh and raring to work."

"Fine by me," Toomey said. "I am beat. And I still have not recovered from that harrowing experience with the moose."

Fargo stripped and tethered the bay. By then Lester had a fire going and Earl was putting coffee on. Fargo placed his saddle and bedroll so his back was to the cliff face and not the aspens. Wearily sitting, he rummaged in his saddlebags for his tin cup.

Toomey was gazing blissfully at the hole. "We're here! Finally and truly here."

"Now comes the hard part," Earl said. "All the digging and the pick work."

"Between what we dig out and Fargo's stake money, I can hire a crew and buy wagons and everything else I need, and in six months the mine will be in operation,"

Toomey predicted. He looked at Fargo. "How does it feel to be rich?"

"I'll tell you once I am."

Toomey chuckled. "You are not one to put the cart before the horse, are you?"

"Not until we know how big the vein is," Fargo said. Some had been known to peter out after a few yards, in which case they would have gone to all this trouble for very little money.

Earl remarked, "A man should always keep a clear head. Speaking of which, one of us has to ride back down the valley in the morning and butcher that moose. Provided a bear or something else doesn't get to it during the night."

"I certainly am not going," Toomey declared.

"Lester and Fargo and me can draw straws," Earl proposed. "Whoever draws the short one cuts up the moose while everyone else stays here and digs."

That is what they did. To make it fair, they had Toomey hold three blades of grass pressed between his fingers with just the ends poking out so they could not tell how long each was, and picked. As whim would have it, Fargo drew the short blade.

"The moose is yours to do," Earl said, "and you are welcome to it. I like fresh meat as much as the next man but I'm not too fond of the blood and gore that goes with carving it up."

"Keep your eyes peeled for that other party we saw," Toomey cautioned. "We don't want them to find us."

"If they do it will be just too bad for them," Lester said. "We are well armed, and it's not like I haven't killed before."

"Hush, you infant," Earl said. "You will have Frank thinking we are cutthroats."

"I would never think that," Toomey assured him. "Not after all you have done for me. You two are about the best friends I have ever had."

"You hear that, Lester?" Earl grinned. "Doesn't it warm the cockles of your heart?"

"What's a cockle?" Lester asked.

When the coffee was ready, Fargo filled his cup and sat back, thinking. He did not like to leave Toomey but it could not be helped. If he insisted he should stay, Earl and Lester might wonder why he was being so pig-headed. Besides, he told himself, whatever happened, Toomey had brought it on himself. There was only so much he could do.

The other three were in good spirits. They joked and laughed, paying no attention to the beastly din that came from down the valley. Fargo paid attention to it. The cries told him the valley was home to wolves and a bear and a female mountain lion that screeched like a woman in labor.

Earl produced a whiskey bottle. "How about a few sips to celebrate? The rest we can save until our packs are crammed with ore."

"Fine by me," Lester said, smacking his lips.

Toomey had reservations. "I guess it can't hurt so long as none of us gets drunk."

Fargo had them add a little to his coffee. A familiar warmth spread down his throat to his belly, and he would have dearly loved to drink more. But a clear head *was* called for.

"What I don't get," Earl commented, "is why the old Indian who brought you here didn't dig out the gold for himself. Most Indians have learned by now how valuable gold is."

"Something else I should have asked him but didn't," Toomey said. "But it honestly never occurred to me."

"The old Indian's loss is our gain," Lester said, then quickly changed it to, "Your gain, I mean, Frank. Yours and Fargo's."

"Lucky them," Earl said.

Fargo was the last to turn in. He did not give in to the demands of his tired body until the others were sound asleep. Now that they had found the gold, he must stay vigilant. That which he expected to happen could happen at any time.

The new day dawned clear and cold. Fargo was the first up and rekindled the fire. He made a fresh pot of coffee. The aroma brought Toomey out of dreamland. Stretching, Toomey smiled at him.

"Good morning. It promises to be a glorious day."

"Don't let it be too glorious," Fargo said.

"I don't understand." Toomey extended an arm toward the hole. "I am on the threshold of having every dream I have ever had come true. How can it be anything less than one of the best days of my life?"

"You are not safe here."

Toomey laughed and said, "Is anyone ever safe anywhere? I refuse to let a little danger spoil my mood."

"The dangers are more than little," Fargo stressed. "And I will be gone most of the day butchering the moose."

"Don't fret on my account," Toomey said. "I'll be fine. Earl and Lester are with me."

"If you do run into trouble," Fargo said, "fire three shots into the air. Sound carries a long way. I should hear, and I will come on the run."

That was when Earl sat up and cast off his blankets. "I don't know if I can get used to this," he said with a yawn. "I like to sleep in until noon."

"You waste half the day that way," Toomey said.

"Show me where it does any harm," Earl said. "My mother was fond of saying the early bird gets the worm but who in hell likes to eat worms except birds?"

Frank Toomey laughed. "I never quite thought of it like that. I have always been an early riser."

So was Fargo. He liked the dawn, liked to see each new day born out of the womb of night. Now he remarked, "I will need to take an extra horse with me to pack in the meat."

"You can take mine," Toomey offered. "I won't have any use for it. I will be busy all day digging."

Fargo left about an hour after sunrise. He had a long day ahead of him and the sooner he got started, the sooner he could get back and keep an eye on Toomey. He cantered for a while and then held the bay to a walk.

The valley pulsed with life. Fargo could not get over

how much of it there was. He had always thought the prairies and the mountains he roamed were abundant with animals of every kind but they were anemic compared to Alaska. It was a Garden of Eden, except that instead of a single serpent to worry about, this Eden was rife with countless creatures that would not hesitate to end his life given half a chance.

Circling vultures were a sign Fargo was getting close. Next he spied a pair of coyotes. They were not at the meat but were standing near a bend and staring hungrily at the feast being denied them. On hearing the horses, they immediately fled. A minute later Fargo drew rein at the same spot.

The moose carcass and the body of the disemboweled horse were where he had last seen them, but they had company. A large black bear, the largest Fargo ever saw, was tearing at the intestines of the stricken horse, its maw buried in the dead animal's innards.

Fargo did not want to kill it if he could help it. Gigging the bay closer, he again drew rein and shucked the Henry. He mentally crossed his fingers that black bears in Alaska were like black bears everywhere, and bellowed, "Ho! Bear! Scat!"

With a loud grunt the black bear pulled its head out of the horse and reared onto its hind legs. It turned its head from side to side but did not spot Fargo until he shouted again.

"Go be a nuisance somewhere else! I have work to do!"

Fargo expected to see it go running off. Instead, it dropped onto all fours and came lumbering toward him, staring fixedly with its ears up in the manner black bears had when they were about to attack.

"Hell," Fargo said. He aimed at the ground in front of the bear. Since he already had a cartridge in the chamber, all he had to do was thumb back the hammer, curl his finger around the trigger, and apply the slightest pressure. At the crack, a dirt geyser spewed over one of the bear's forepaws. The bear stopped and reared.

Fargo centered the Henry's sights on its throat. Given his druthers he would let the bear live. He waited for it to do something but all it did was stare.

Suddenly the black bear opened its mouth and growled. Fargo construed that as a prelude to rushing him, but as if to prove the axiom that bears were the most unpredictable creatures on God's green earth, the black bear dropped onto all fours, wheeled, and vanished into the forest.

Fargo stayed where he was a while, to be safe. At length he gigged the bay forward.

The dead horse showed signs of swelling and the odor it gave off was far from pleasant. Loosening his bandanna, Fargo pulled it up over his mouth and nose, then retightened the knot. It kept out the worst of the stench, which would be considerably worse in a few days.

Since they had no need for the hide, Fargo did not skin the moose as he would if they intended to use it. He started by cutting down the hind legs, making a single cut from the tail to the chin, and then slicing a line up the inside of each front leg. From that point he peeled the hide from the body, using the knife only when the membranes proved stubborn.

The hide was still pliable but not nearly as manageable as it would be if cured. He cut it into thirds and set the sections aside with the hair facing down. The next step was to carve up the meat. He could not take it all. He chose the softer, choice parts, which on a moose were not as tender as, say, the choicest parts of a cow but were nowhere near as lean as the meat on, say, a mountain goat.

It was hard work. His toothpick was sharp but there were a lot of tendons and bones to deal with. He became so engrossed that he paid no heed to the passage of time. He did have the presence of mind to scan the valley now and again for sign of anything that might be inclined to do him harm.

As it was, by the clock it would be pushing four in the afternoon when Fargo tied the last of the bundles onto Toomey's horse and stepped back with a nod of satisfaction. He would take the meat back and in the morning slice it into strips so it could be hung over racks and dried.

Fargo walked to the stream and knelt to wash his hands. They were caked with blood and other internal juices and smelled almost as bad as the dead horse. He dipped his hands in the cold water and rubbed his fingers and palms. His reflection stared back at him.

Seconds later, so did another.

Men had come out of the spruce on the other side of the stream and one of them came to the edge of the bank and smiled down at him.

"Surprised to see me, American?" Vassily Baranof asked.

9

Fargo calmly finished washing his hands and wiped them on his buckskin pants. Slowly rising, he returned Vassily's smug smile with his own. "I am not surprised at all, Russian," he answered. "Truth is, I was wondering why you were taking so long."

"You have been expecting me? I find that hard to believe." Vassily motioned, and half of the eighteen men who had come out of the woods with him turned and went back in. The rest warily converged, their rifles leveled.

"I saw your face in the Motherland when Toomey mentioned the gold," Fargo said. "As we Americans like to say, you wear your greed on your sleeve."

"Or you are more observant than most," Vassily said. "But not so observant that you saw us creep up on you."

"Is that what you were doing?" Fargo retorted. "The way your men were clumping around, I figured you didn't care if I knew."

The big Russian laughed. "You fight with words as superbly as you do with your fists." He pointed at the Colt. "Which makes me suspect you are also skilled with your revolver. Hand it over, if you please, and even if you do not."

With all those rifles pointed at him it would be suicide to resist. Fargo carefully drew the Colt and just as carefully held it out. "I never argue with a gent who has a private army."

The big Russian jumped the stream in a long bound and relieved Fargo of his six-shooter. "You amuse me. I think I will keep you alive a while yet."

"Until you have the gold, anyway," Fargo said.

"Oh, I know where it is," Vassily taunted. "One of my men is watching your friends as we speak."

"Acquaintances."

"Eh? Are you suggesting you are not on good terms with them? Why, then, did they bring you to the gold?"

"I own a half-interest," Fargo revealed.

"A half-interest in nothing," Vassily corrected him, "since soon it will be mine."

Other members of the party were crossing the stream. Those who had entered the woods were reemerging with mounts and pack animals. To Fargo's considerable surprise, two of the figures on horseback were women. "You brought everything a person needs, I see."

Misunderstanding, Vassily said, "Nine packhorses with enough food and ammunition to last us indefinitely. I am always prepared. It is why I have lasted so long at what I do."

"What would that be? Besides breaking the law?"

Vassily's grin was the grin of a bobcat about to pounce on a sparrow. "You sound like Captain Petrov. And like the conscientious captain, you fail to grasp that for some of us, laws are at best an inconvenience. I have never lived by the rules imposed on us by our so-called betters. I am above that."

"Or below it," Fargo said. He glimpsed movement and sidestepped a punch that would have landed solidly on his jaw. He raised his own fists but froze at the click of multiple rifle hammers.

"No!" Vassily commanded. "He is not to be killed until I say he is to be killed." To Fargo he said, "You amuse me, yes, but I have a low tolerance for insults. You would do well to keep that in mind."

Loud splashing erupted as the riders crossed the stream. Among them were the two women, who reined up on either side of Vassily Baranof. On the right was a black-haired beauty in a heavy coat, long skirt, and high boots. "Introduce me to your handsome friend, brother."

Vassily motioned at Fargo and chuckled. "An *acquaintance*, sister. I call him American to annoy him. American, permit me to introduce Sabina Baranof, my sister, and her best friend, Kira Ivanov."

The best friend was a stunning brunette with lively green eyes, full lips like ripe strawberries, and an exquisite shape her loose-fitting clothes could not conceal. She smiled at Fargo and said in throaty English, "I am much pleased to you meet, American."

"You must excuse her," Vassily said. "Her English is atrocious. Few in Sitka are as fluent as my sister and I, but then, we had a private tutor. A benefit of being a Baranof."

Sabina lithely dismounted and boldly walked up to Fargo, appraising him as she might a stallion she was interested in buying. "It puzzles me that my brother did not have you shot on sight. What did you do that he admires you so?"

"I hit him," Fargo said.

"You must hit hard. He has only contempt for those who are weak and craven." Sabina offered her slender hand. "I share that trait."

Her grip was stronger than that of many men. Fargo met her frank scrutiny with his own, letting his gaze linger at her bosom, and lower down.

"Do you like what you see?" Sabina teased.

Vassily glowered his disapproval. "Must you throw yourself at every man who interests you? Can't you control your urges for once and pretend you are not a wanton minx?"

"Why, brother," Sabina said. "That is one of the nicest compliments you have ever paid me." She leaned close to Fargo. "He does not like to be reminded that he is not the only black sheep in our family."

Kira Ivanof had also climbed down. She smoothed her dress and, whether by design or accident, displayed quite nice legs to go with her quite nice bosom. "You eat me with your eyes," she said, and she was not displeased.

"To a man who is starved every woman is a feast."

Kira and Sabina both laughed, and the latter whispered something to her brother, who did not find it nearly as amusing.

"You have made quite an impression, American. It is unfortunate I must eventually kill you." Vassily pivoted toward his men, and suddenly he was authority personified, barking orders like a military commander. In short order everyone was mounted in pairs, with the two women behind Vassily and Fargo. At a wave of Vassily's arm the entire column started up the valley.

"There is one thing I do not know but would very much like to," Vassily said. "Specifically, how much gold is there?"

"You are asking the wrong man," Fargo said. "I came after the moose meat while the rest stayed to dig."

"You came all this way and you truly do not know? That does not strike me as being very intelligent."

"I've had brighter ideas," Fargo said.

"About the meat," Vassily remarked, "I feel a celebration is in order tonight. I trust you will not mind if your moose is the main course."

"Not so long as I'm alive to eat some of it," Fargo said.

The Russian gave a hearty laugh. "It will truly be a pity when I have you staked out and gutted."

"In America we give the condemned a last request."

"Then I can do no less. What is your request? What would you ask of me?" Vassily asked.

"That I'm not staked out and gutted."

More laughter ensued, and Vassily twisted in the saddle to say, "Did you hear him, sister? Where others would cringe and beg for their lives, he meets every thrust with a counterthrust."

"He must be quite the swordsman," Sabina said.

Fargo was honest with her. "I've hardly ever held one unless you count a cavalry saber."

"That is not the kind of sword I had in mind," Sabina

enlightened him with an impish grin. "My brother must keep you alive long enough for me to find out if the tales about Americans are true."

"Tales?" Fargo said.

"About American—how do you say it?—prowess?"

Kira giggled. "Like on a ship? No pants can be big enough."

Vassily swore in English and Russian. "Do you see what I must put up with?" he said to Fargo. Then, over his shoulder to the women, "It is the custom for those of one country to weave tales about those of another. The English do it with the French and the French do it with the Africans. Men from another country are always bigger than the men from their own. Women from another country are always tigresses in bed. That sort of nonsense."

"It would still be fun to find out," Sabina said.

"Women," Vassily sniffed.

"Yes, women," Fargo said, "and you brought them out here, of all places. That does not strike me as being very intelligent," he mimicked Vassily's earlier comment.

"You think it stupid of me. But you try to say no to my sister. It cannot be done." Swiveling at the hips, Vassily swept an arm along the long line of riders. "But I did bring, as you put it, my own army with me so they would be well protected."

"Oh, my brother is very protective," Sabina said. "Too much so at times."

"Brothers be too bossy," Kira added.

Vassily was even less amused. "Is this the thanks I get for doing my best to keep you from being harmed? Is this the thanks I get for caring?"

Sabina laughed that gay laugh of hers. "Listen to him, Kira. We have hurt his feelings. Now he will pout for a while and later he will apologize for being such a boor."

"I very love boar meat," Kira said.

"Not that kind of boar, dear," Sabina said.

And so it went, the two women prattling on with occasional comments from Vassily as they wound deeper into the valley. After a while Fargo shut out the gab. He had weightier issues to grapple with. Foremost among them was how to stay alive. He was still breathing only because Vassily enjoyed toying with him. Their game of cat and mouse could turn deadly at any moment.

Then there was Frank Toomey. Fargo would like to save him, if he could. Earl and Lester were another matter. They claimed to be Toomey's friends, but if Fargo was any judge of character, they were wolves in smelly sheep's clothing.

Vassily's party was approximately a quarter of a mile from the end of the valley when he rose in the stirrups and raised an arm to bring the column to a halt. Dismounting, he snapped commands in Russian.

Fargo stayed on the bay. He was hoping to make a break but two men with rifles came and covered him, one telling him in heavily accented English to climb down.

Half the Russians were to stay with the horses. The rest, and the women, were to accompany Vassily. He had his men advance in a skirmish line, with himself, the women, and Fargo at the center.

"From here on, no one is to speak. That includes you, my sister. There are three more Americans and they have guns, and I would be quite annoyed if I am shot because you cannot keep that mouth of yours shut."

"Why, brother"—Sabina pretended to be stricken by his barb—"when have I ever not listened to you?"

"Only all the time," Vassily said.

"Your brother is much the man," Kira said to Sabina, and both laughed.

"So is my sister," Vassily said coldly. "And I will remind you not to remind me of that. There is only so much I will let my nose be rubbed in. Now quiet, the both of you."

For once the women listened.

Fargo was next to Sabina. A pine rose in front of them and she swung around it to the left as he was doing, her arm and leg brushing his. He soon noticed that she contrived to rub against him every chance she got. It occurred to him that he should encourage her interest for his own ends. With that in mind, when they had strayed a few yards from Vassily and he could whisper without being heard, he leaned toward her and said in her ear, "You are quite lovely."

Sabina glowed like a lit lantern and purred, "How sweet. I was beginning to think you did not like me."

"I do not want your brother mad at me," Fargo said.

"He will not touch you so long as I do not want him to," Sabina whispered. "And I will not want him to so long as you do that which pleases me."

"How can we?" Fargo asked. "He will keep me under guard."

"I am a woman. I have my wiles," Sabina boasted. "When night comes I will see what I can do."

Fargo grimly smiled. They were much alike, brother and sister. Both were arrogant and vicious, human vipers with venomous fangs they would sink into him at his first lapse in judgment. He must watch what he said and did.

As if to prove his point, Vassily suddenly veered toward them and snapped, "What were you and my sister whispering about?"

Sabina answered before Fargo could think up a suitable reply. "He warned me to stay low if shooting starts. Was that not thoughtful of him, my brother?"

Vassily snorted. "You do think me a fool. But no matter. When I said no talking, I meant no talking. Not one word from either of you or you will see a side of me that is most unpleasant. You have seen that side before, my sister. Remember?"

Sabina flushed red but did not say anything.

Cupping a hand to his ear, Vassily said, "I did not hear you." Grinning, he moved off.

"He presumes too much," Sabina said so only Fargo heard her. "One day he will go too far."

The stand of aspens appeared. Vassily signaled for his men to halt and glanced about as if looking for something or someone. Momentarily, another Russian came cat-footing toward them. Fargo guessed it was the man Vassily had sent to keep watch over Toomey, Earl, and Lester. Whatever the man told Vassily caused him to motion for the skirmish line to form into a crescent. Vassily gave instructions for the women to stay where they were, and for Fargo to stay with them, leaving two men to guard him.

The Russians began to close in.

Fargo expected an outcry or a shot. Earl and Lester, if not the timid Toomey, were bound to resist.

Suddenly, after taking only a few steps, the Russians stopped.

Earl had come out of the aspens. He was smiling, and holding his rifle over his head with both hands. Heedless of the muzzles pointed at him, he nonchalantly strolled up to Vassily Baranof.

"About time you got here."

10

To judge by the reactions of some of the Russians, Fargo was not the only one who was surprised.

Vassily Baranof looked the pudgy bundle of filth up and down, his features curling in distaste. "Do I know you?"

"We've never met, no, but I know you. Or all about you, rather," Earl said glibly. "You are the king of the Sitka underworld. Nothing underhanded happens that you don't have your fingers in."

"What you say is true," Vassily conceded. At a flick of his finger, one of his men relieved Earl of his rifle. "It is also common knowledge, and does not explain how you greeted me."

"It's simple, Mr. Baranof," Earl said. "Me and my partner would like to work for you."

"The more you say, the more you confuse me," Vassily responded. "I am not here to offer employment. I am here to kill you and anyone else who stands in my way, and claim the gold for my own."

Earl showed his discolored teeth in a broad smile. "No need to rub out anyone. My partner and me have already taken care of Frank Toomey, the gent who filed the claim. The gold is all yours."

Concern spiked through Fargo. "What did you do to him?"

Earl chuckled. "Relax. He's not dead. Lester and me jumped him and Lester held him down while I trussed him for Mr. Baranof, here. He's lying back there whining about how mean we are."

Vassily held up a hand and Earl instantly fell silent. "Am I to understand that you have been expecting me to show up? That you have bound Mr. Toomey as a gesture of good will toward me?"

"You've hit the nail on the head," Earl said, nodding enthusiastically. "That's exactly what we did."

"Back up again. How, exactly, did you know that *I* was following you?"

"We knew someone was," Earl said. "We spotted your party a couple of times. Frank had told me about what happened in the Motherland, so it wasn't hard to figure out you would be interested."

"Remarkable," Vassily said. "You do not appear to have the intellect of a gnat."

"My partner and me can be of use to you," Earl said confidently.

Vassily adopted a superior smirk. "You are aware, I trust, that all those who work for me are Russian? That I regard Americans for the most part as pigs or cretins or both?" He looked Earl up and down again. "You, by the way, are a sterling example of the qualities I most despise about your kind."

"I've heard you tend to look down your nose at those of us who aren't from Mother Russia, yes," Earl admitted. "But I've also heard that while you don't hire Americans outright, you do have some who work for you. You pay them to report anything of interest in the American sector."

"You are remarkably well informed," Vassily said. "I have kept my liaisons with your countrymen a secret."

"One of them talked in his cups," Earl revealed. "It got me to thinking."

"That you can do that amazes me no end."

"Do what?" Earl asked.

"Think."

Slapping his thigh, Earl laughed uproariously. "That

was a good one, Mr. Baranof, sir. If you will let me take you to our camp, I have coffee on, and I'd imagine you want to see the gold."

"Not so fast," Vassily snapped. "Something about this does not ring true."

It did not ring true with Fargo, either. Earl had no way of knowing Baranof would show up when he did. Which meant Earl and Lester had another reason for jumping Toomey and tying him up.

Vassily half turned. "What say you, sister? Do I have him shot where he stands?"

The women had been unusually quiet during the exchange. Sabina stepped next to her brother and regarded Earl much as Vassily had done. "He is hideous. He reeks of foul odors. His clothes have never been washed. He is the most abominable person I have ever met."

"Begging your pardon, ma'am," Earl said. "But you haven't met Lester yet. He has me beat all hollow."

"Remarkable," Vassily said again.

Kira, holding her nose, had gone over. "You slay me with your stink. How can you breathe yourself?"

Earl sniffed his armpit. "I reckon I'm used to me, ma'am."

"Have you never heard of hot water and soap?" Sabina asked.

"Yes, ma'am. But my mother always warned us kids that baths makes us puny and sickly. So I don't generally take one but once every couple of years or so."

Vassily seemed more fascinated than repulsed. "What is your name, pigman?"

"Marsten, sir. Earl Marsten. My partner's name is Lester Deeter. He's watching Toomey for you."

"You may accompany us," Vassily informed him. "But you will not speak unless spoken to and, whatever you do, do not let me inhale your odor unless I bid you to come close."

"Whatever you say, Mr. Baranof, sir." Earl smiled and came and stood next to Fargo.

Another Russian joined the two already covering

Fargo and pointed his rifle at Earl's back. At a signal from Vassily the rest started forward.

One of the men behind Fargo prodded him with his rifle. "Go easy with that thing." He glanced at the trio of bearded huskies. "Do any of you speak English?"

None of them answered.

"This is a fine kettle of fish," Earl said. "You go off to fetch moose meat and come back with a pack of killers."

"A minute ago you were fit to lick Baranof's boots," Fargo noted.

"I would do most anything to keep from being turned into a sieve," Earl quietly replied. "I was in the aspens, waiting for you to come back, when I saw Vassily and his boys ride up. I tell you, I did some fast thinking."

"Why were you waiting for me?"

Earl looked away. "I figured you would need help with the meat."

Fargo wasn't fooled. Earl and Lester had planned to kill him and keep the gold for themselves. "You don't really want to work for Baranof?"

"You heard him. He thinks I'm a pig. Him and his sister putting on airs like they did." Earl caught himself and glanced at the guards, then lowered his voice. "We are in a fix, no two ways about it. We have to work together or we are both goners."

"Don't forget Toomey and Lester," Fargo said.

"I would never forget Lester. Him and me have been pards since I came west ten years ago. He is like a brother to me."

"Why is it I can't tell when you are telling the truth and when you are lying through your teeth?"

Earl swore. "Fine. Treat me no better than the Russian. But there are twenty of them and only four of us."

The devil of it was, Fargo reflected, Earl had a point. Alone, none of them stood a chance. Combined, they might make it out alive.

The fire was crackling, the horses were grazing undisturbed. Lester was drinking coffee. At the sight of them, he promptly stood and held his arms out from his sides to demonstrate he did not have a gun.

Frank Toomey lay on his side, his wrists bound behind his back and his ankles tied. He glared at Earl Marsten. "So this is why you hog-tied me? You are in cahoots with these Russians?"

Vassily Baranof did not break stride. He walked up to Toomey and kicked him in the ribs. "I do not like your tone."

Toomey could not reply. He was thrashing and sputtering, his face a beet-red mask of pain.

Vassily turned to Lester and regarded him with revulsion. "I did not believe it possible, but you are uglier and filthier than your friend."

Lester glanced at Earl, who said, "Thank the man for the compliment, Lester. You and me might be working for him soon."

"Thank you, Mr. Baranof, for saying as how I am as dirty as sin," Lester said.

Vassily glanced at his sister. "Can it be?"

"They must be shamming," Sabina said. "No one could be this stupid."

Thoughtfully scratching his beard, Vassily said, "It is easy to determine. Mr. Deeter, would you stick your right hand in the fire for me."

"Huh?" Lester said.

"Your right hand. I would like to see it burn," Vassily explained. "Do me this favor and I will take you and your friend under my wing, as you Americans are fond of saying."

Lester held up his right hand and wriggled his fingers. "But I'm fond of this hand. I've had it since I was a baby."

"Do it, Lester," Earl urged.

"Like hell I will," Lester snapped. "This was your brainstorm. Stick your own damn hand in the fire."

"He asked you to," Earl said.

"Well, he can just unask me, then," Lester declared.

Vassily was staring from one to the other and grinning. "Am I to take it, then, Mr. Deeter, that you refuse?

What if I tell you that if you do not stick your hand in the fire, I will point at one of my men and he will shoot you in the head?"

"Then you are the stupid one," Lester said.

"In what regard, Mr. Deeter?"

"I'd be little use to you with only one hand and no use to you dead," Lester said. "You Russians. You're as dumb as tree stumps."

"One of us is," Vassily Baranof said. He pointed at a stocky underling with the neck and shoulders of a bull. "Pyotr, show this pig what we think of Americans who think Russians are as dumb as tree stumps. And do it without spattering blood over the rest of us."

Lester backed up a step. "Now you just hold on, mister. You can't have me shot for saying my piece."

"Actually, yes, I can," Vassily replied, and nodded at Pyotr.

The stocky Russian sank to one knee and angled his rifle up at Lester. He showed no more emotion than a rock as he sighted along the barrel and fired. The heavy slug cored Lester's forehead smack in the center and blew out the rear of his skull in a spectacular shower of scarlet, hair, bone, and brain. The body swayed like a reed in the wind, then crashed to earth in the fire. Burning brands arced every which way. Sabina and Kira leaped back, as did several of the men. But not Vassily. He leaned down, grabbed hold of Lester's coat, and hauled him from the flames.

"Pyotr, have the body disposed of. Whoever you pick must take it off and bury it deep enough that we will not have to deal with scavengers."

"Your will." Pyotr acknowledged the order with a bow.

Vassily faced Earl. "Which brings us to you. You say that you would like to work for me? Prove it. Do what your friend would not. Put your hand in the fire and keep it there until I say you can take it out."

"But, Mr. Baranof," Earl started to object. He was gaping at Lester.

"Would you rather I have Pyotr shoot you as he did your friend?" Vassily demanded.

"Lester was my best friend," Earl said.

"What is that to me?" Vassily snapped. "All I care about is being obeyed. You claim that you would like to work for me, but here you are, about to make the same mistake he did."

Earl tore his shocked gaze from Lester's lifeless form and moved to the fire. Squatting, he thrust his right hand into the flames. A grimace twisted his countenance.

Kira Ivanov tittered and covered her mouth and nose. "Everything is smells today."

Vassily said a few words in Russian and a man seized Earl and flung him from the fire so roughly, Earl tumbled onto his back. "That is enough. You have proven yourself."

Earl was gritting his teeth. His fingers were singed in spots but he had not suffered irreparable harm.

"We will discuss your future later," Vassily informed him. "Right now I would very much like to see the gold I have gone to such time and expense and personal discomfort to acquire." His finger rose and pointed at Fargo. "You will do the honors."

In Fargo's absence someone had covered the hole with the lattice. Lifting it, he set it aside and stepped back.

Vassily dropped to his hands and knees. So did Sabina and Kira.

"It certainly looks like gold," the sister said. "But what if it is not? What if it is what they call fool's gold?"

"That is why I brought Fedor," Vassily said, and snapped his fingers while uttering a string of Russian.

A skinny man with no chin came from behind the others. In contrast to the rest he was clean shaven. Another contrast were his clothes; he wore a suit where the others preferred wool shirts and heavy pants. He had a small black bag similar to the bag a doctor might carry. He spoke in Russian.

"Use English," Vassily directed. "The Americans should hear since their lives hang on the thread of your decision."

"As you wish," Fedor said.

"You know what is required. Get to it."

"Immediately." Fedor stepped to the edge and dropped into the hole. He set his bag down. Kneeling, he ran a hand over the vein. "Promising. Most promising." He opened his bag and took out a small wooden box. Inside the box were vials and chemicals. "For testing the gold," he said when Fargo's curiosity got the better of him.

Fargo was impressed. "Where did you find a chemist on such short notice?" he asked Baranof.

"Fedor is on my payroll. For testing coins and jewelry and the like." Vassily smiled. "As I told you before, I am always prepared, American. For every contingency. It is why I will die an old man in a rocking chair."

No sooner were the words out of his mouth than an arrow sailed out of the blue and thudded into the earth next to him.

11

Everyone was caught by surprise. Everyone stared at the arrow as if they could not quite credit their senses. Then Vassily Baranof heaved erect and bawled commands. Instantly, a knot of men with rifles surrounded the two women and hurried them into the aspens. Other men raised their rifles to the cliff and the adjoining slopes.

Fargo had already dropped into a crouch and was scanning the vicinity but saw no one. He had a fair notion where the arrow came from, based on its angle of flight, but no bowman was visible. Whoever let the shaft fly had seemingly vanished without a trace.

Of all of them, only the chemist, Fedor, went on with what he was doing, undisturbed by the excitement.

Frank Toomey could not take cover, even though his fear-struck expression suggested he dearly yearned to do so. "Help me!" he yelled to Fargo. "Get me into the trees!"

"You are fine right where you are," Fargo said, straightening.

"But the arrow!"

"Thanks for reminding me," Fargo said dryly, and picked the arrow up. Right away he noticed two things. First, the arrow had been made recently. If he had to guess, he would say it had been fashioned in the past month or so. The condition of the shaft, of the sinew that bound the sharp iron tip to the shaft, and of the feathers, all showed the arrow had not been used much, if at all. Second, the arrow bore no markings. None whatsoever. The shaft was plain wood. Which was strange. It was customary for tribes to paint symbols on their arrows, or notch or groove them in some distinctive way that enabled those familiar with the markings to tell which tribe made it.

The shaft was suddenly snatched from Fargo's hand. Vassily Baranof examined it, then growled in Russian and handed it to another man. "This is Mishka. He knows more about the Indians of this region than anyone."

Mishka had a high forehead and wide-set eyes, and was clearly as puzzled as Fargo had been. He addressed Vassily in Russian.

"He says he cannot tell which tribe made the arrow," Vassily translated. He issued more orders and half a dozen of his hirelings spread out and churned up the slopes.

The women came out of the aspens, Sabina saying, "It must be an Indian boy playing a prank, brother."

"No." Vassily wagged the arrow. "Did you not notice that it was me this almost struck? Whoever loosed it at us wanted me dead."

"But who?" Sabina asked.

"Need I remind you we have made many enemies, sister?" Vassily said.

"Need I remind you most of them are dead?" Sabina rejoined. "And none are Indians."

"True," Vassily said, clearly more perplexed than ever. He watched the men above conduct their search. When one turned and yelled down to him, he swore and beckoned for them to come back down.

"He says there is no sign of anyone," Vassily relayed for Fargo's benefit. "He says they cannot even find footprints."

"The ground is hard and rocky."

"Even so," Vassily said. He handed the arrow to Pyotr. "Put it in one of the packs. We will take it back with us and show it around. Maybe someone will have an answer."

"At once," Pyotr said.

Fedor, the chemist, looked up from his vials and chemicals. "It will be a while before my tests are complete but I have seen enough to say I am positive this is gold."

"Finish your tests." Vassily gazed at the western sky, at the bloodred sun low on the horizon. "In the morning I will have the men dig. I must find out whether I have a true vein or a pocket."

"Do you still plan to have your feast?" Fargo asked.

"Why wouldn't I?" Vassily said. "Because of the arrow? I am not easily scared. I will post guards, and we will make several fires to keep the dark at bay."

"Maybe the arrow was not meant for you," Fargo said. "Maybe it was a warning."

"From a local tribe? That we are in their territory and must leave?" Vassily nodded. "That occurred to me. But if so, I must disappoint them. I am not leaving until I have enough gold to make me the richest man in Mother Russia."

"The gold is that important to you?"

"It is my salvation. I was driven from Russia by certain government officials who took a dim view of my activities. They wanted to put me in prison and throw away the key. Me! Vassily Baranof! But I will show them. With enough gold I can buy them off or ruin them. I will be able to go back. To live where and as I please." Vassily gazed at the hole. "Yes, American, the gold is important to me."

So it was not just greed, Fargo thought to himself. He was about to ask about the officials who had driven Baranof from the motherland when several men came running up. They bowed their heads, and whatever report one of their number gave Vassily caused him to clench his fists and hiss between clenched teeth.

"What now?"

"The pudgy one, Earl. The one with the glib tongue. He has disappeared. In the confusion he slipped away and my men cannot find him."

"Slipped away or was taken," Fargo suggested.

Vassily stiffened. "Yes. There is that possibility." He growled more instructions and the men departed. "This affair is becoming more complicated than I would like."

"I know the feeling," Fargo said.

The Russians who had been scouring the slopes returned. Two were left at the hole with the chemist. Everyone else retired through the aspens to where tents were being erected and the horses picketed. Whatever else might be said of Baranof, everything he did, he did well.

Fargo was left by one of the tents, under guard. He was not alone. Toomey was dumped beside him and wasted no time in complaining.

"This is terrible. Just terrible. Poor Lester killed! Earl missing. What are we to do?"

"Nothing."

Toomey was flabbergasted. "How can you say that? Any moment, that crazy Russian might take it into his head to have us murdered like he did Lester."

"Baranof is as sane as you or me," Fargo said.

"You're defending him? My God. After he has stolen the gold out from under us."

Fargo changed the subject. "Did you see any Indians when you were up here before?"

"Besides old Gray Fox? No. I asked him if there were any villages nearby and he said the Tlingits hunt elk in this area now and then, and that was it."

"The Tlingits are a coast tribe," Fargo remembered.

"A whole bunch of tribes—or, rather, clans, I guess we would call them. From what Gray Fox told me, the clans are formed into two big societies, the Wolf and the Raven. He was a Wolf. He added some nonsense about the Wolves taking on the traits of real wolves and the Ravens having the qualities of real ravens. Typical Indian superstition."

"Do the Tlingits use bows?"

"Not very often, no. They are fishermen, mostly. They have knives and clubs and spears and the like." Toomey paused. "Why do you ask? That arrow?"

Fargo shrugged. "I was just curious."

"It was probably a hunter from some other tribe," Toomey speculated. "A white-hater who is halfway back to his village by now."

"Could be," Fargo said.

Presently eight tents had been erected and several campfires were blazing. The moose meat was cut up and skewered on spits to roast. Tea was put on to brew. Russians, Fargo had discovered, were more fond of tea than coffee. Tripods with heavy pots were used to boil potatoes, corn, and sugar beets.

Quiet fell as everyone settled down for the evening meal.

Vassily posted sentries, telling Fargo he had given orders to shoot anything that moves. "That includes Earl Marsten. I do not know why he ran off unless he was afraid I would have him shot as I did his friend, but he has made me angry. Which is not wise to do."

"What about me?" Fargo asked.

"What about you?" Vassily retorted. "Eat, drink, and be merry, for tomorrow you may die." He smiled as he said it but there was no doubt he meant it.

"And Frank there?" Fargo asked, nodding at Toomey.

"I do not like him as I like you," Vassily said. "He will stay tied."

Toomey had heard, and objected. "What if I give you my word I won't try to run off? Please. My arms and legs are cramping. I can barely wriggle my fingers, the circulation has been cut off for so long."

"Ask me if I care, American, and I will tell you I don't," Vassily replied. "The only reason you are still breathing is because I have special plans for the two of you."

"What sort of plans?"

"You must wait until morning to find out," Vassily answered. "But I will have you untied so you may eat and drink. I may be cruel, as some claim, but I try to observe the amenities. More than that, you must not expect."

"It's not fair," Toomey said. "I have never done anything to you."

"You are an American and that is enough."

"Why?" Toomey asked, his voice rising. "What did Americans ever do that you hate us so much?"

"A good question," Vassily said. "I will humor you and share a story which Fargo might find interesting as well." He paused. "It is not just that Americans are slovenly. It is not just that Americans think they are better than everyone else—"

"I never do that," Toomey broke in. "Neither does Fargo. You can't judge all Americans by the actions of a few."

Vassily rose, took a couple of steps, and smashed his heel down on Toomey's leg. Toomey cried out and rolled back and forth, spittle dribbling over his lower lip. When he subsided and lay gasping, Vassily told him, "Kindly do not interrupt me again. It is rude. And for your information, I will judge Americans and anyone else as I see fit. Understood?"

Toomey was in too much pain to reply.

"Now where was I?" Vassily sat back down. "Oh, yes. When I first came to Sitka, I approached the American consul about becoming an American citizen. Yes, me, Vassily Baranof. If I were an American citizen, the Russian government could not touch me for crimes I committed in Russia. I could start over." Vassily's tone grew flinty. "But it was not to be. The American government checked my background. They found out about some of my ventures that were not aboveboard, as one lackey put it. So they refused to grant me citizenship. They refused to even let me into their country."

"You are a criminal," Toomey said. "What else did you expect?"

"I will enjoy killing you," Vassily said. "You are one of those who does not know when to keep his mouth shut."

"You noticed that, too?" Fargo said.

A Russian at the next fire called out, and Vassily rose

again. "You must excuse me. I have certain arrangements to make."

Fargo was about to stand and go to Toomey when the warm pressure of a hand on his arm stopped him.

"Here you are. Kira and I have been looking for you," Sabina Baranof declared. "If I did not know better, I would think you were avoiding us."

The women had freshened up and brushed their hair. Both were more than uncommonly lovely, their full bosoms and luscious red lips enough to stir any man.

"What do you have in mind?" Fargo asked.

"We would like the pleasure of your company," Sabina said. "Agree to sit with us while we eat, and afterward we will go on a stroll."

"All three of us?"

Sabina laughed. "Kira and I will toss a coin when the meal is over. You will have the honor of being alone with the winner."

"I hope it be me," Kira said.

"Your brother might have something to say about that," Fargo said to Sabina.

"Leave Vassily to me. He never denies me anything."

The Russians were talking and joking and laughing. They were relaxed, at ease, apparently unconcerned about the arrow or Earl's absence. They passed around a flask of vodka. Vassily permitted each a few sips.

The cook announced that the food was done and began heaping it on plates. Sabina took one of Fargo's arms and Kira the other, and they guided him to a fire and sank to the ground, tugging him down with them. They sat so close that their arms and legs rubbed him when either of them moved.

"Are you hungry, handsome one?" Sabina asked. "We always eat well. My brother insists on it. There is a Russian saying." She stopped, her forehead puckered. "How does it go in English? If the stomach is happy, so is the man."

A plate was set in Fargo's lap and he was handed a knife and fork. The moose meat was sizzling hot. The potatoes, the corn, and the beets were done to perfection.

Vassily gave a speech in Russian. Midway through, Sabina leaned over to Fargo, her breath warm on his neck, and whispered, "He is thanking them for their hard work. He says that if the vein of gold is as rich as he hopes it is, everyone will be paid a bonus." She winked at him. "That brother of mine, he knows how to win men over." Grinning, she brazenly placed her hand on Fargo's inner thigh. "For that matter, so do I."

Fargo indicated the two men who constantly covered him. "I still don't see how you aim to pull it off."

"Have you never heard of feminine wiles?" Sabina grinned. "Before this night is done, I will have my way with you."

12

For dessert they were served pudding. Fargo had eaten so much moose meat he was full, but Sabina and Kira helped themselves to generous portions. Kira, in particular, had an appetite worthy of a lumberjack. When Fargo remarked on how much she ate, she smiled and patted her stomach.

"Russian women have much big bellies."

At that Sabina laughed. "I really must help her improve her English."

After the meal several of Vassily's men were given the chore of washing the dishes and pots. The women did not offer to help. In fact, when Sabina handed her plate over, she joked to Kira. "It sure is nice to have men around. They do all the work while we take it easy."

"You never lend a hand?" Fargo asked.

"Who in their right mind wants to do dishes?" Sabina rejoined. "In Russia I always had servants do the menial work. In Sitka it is the same." She patted her friend's hand. "Kira is not as well off and has to do her own. I have helped her a few times, and I can say that cleaning is a drudge. I would rather have my teeth pulled."

Despite himself, Fargo smiled.

The Russians were a bundle of surprises. After dessert they sat around the campfires singing Russian folk songs.

The women joined in the singing, but not Vassily. He sat aloof from the rest.

It was no later than ten when Sabina took a Russian coin from a leather pouch she wore around her waist, and held the coin for Kira to see. Kira said a single word in Russian. Sabina nodded and flipped the coin. She did not catch it but let it land on the ground. Both eagerly sat forward to see the result, and Sabina scowled.

"Two out of three," she said in English.

Kira reluctantly nodded.

Sabina flipped the coin again, and yet a third time, and sat back beaming. "You are mine tonight," she said to Fargo.

Kira looked so crestfallen that when Sabina was not looking, Fargo gave her thigh a pinch. She grinned and stared at a spot below his belt. The invitation was clear.

About that time two men got up and began to dance. They folded their arms in front of them and kicked out with their legs, hopping like oversized rabbits in time to the singing. Others clapped and cheered them on.

Fargo felt a hand slip into his own. He did not resist when Sabina pulled him to his feet and led him to one of the larger tents. Opening the flap, she motioned for him to precede her.

"This is mine and Kira's. No one would dare set foot in it except my brother." Sabina closed the flap and began tying it shut so they would not be intruded on.

The interior was dark as pitch. Fargo's eyes slowly adjusted, enabling him to make out blankets to his left.

Sabina sashayed toward them. "I trust you can undress without a light on."

"I've had a little practice," Fargo said.

Grinning, Sabina stopped and turned and hungrily molded her body to his, her fingers rising to clasp his neck and pull his mouth down to hers. "Kiss me, handsome one. I have thought of nothing but your kisses all day."

Fargo obliged. Her lips were exquisitely soft. They parted to admit his tongue and hers swirled around his. At the same time he reached behind her and cupped her bottom. Grinding his manhood into her, he elicited a soft moan.

"You kiss nicely," Sabina said when they broke for breath. "I tingle down to my toes."

Fargo kissed her again, his hands rising to her breasts. Even through her dress he felt how hard her nipples became. They were tacks against his palms. He pinched them, provoking a gasp, and sculpted each full globe. Soon she was panting into his mouth and grinding her hips against him. When she finally stepped back, her eyelids were hooded and her bosom was rising and falling excitedly.

"I like you more and more, handsome one," Sabina said throatily. "It will be a shame if Vassily has you killed."

Fargo did not care to be reminded. To shut her up he looped his arm around her hips and pulled her to him. Their next kiss went on and on. Her tongue was velvet need. Meanwhile her fingers explored his body. He stirred low down. He did more than stir when she abruptly cupped him and stroked his manhood. He grew rock hard.

"My goodness. You are a stallion," Sabina said.

"You talk too much." Scooping her into his arms, Fargo lowered her onto the blankets. She smiled languidly and crooked her leg in sensual invitation.

"Like what you see?"

The devil of it was, Fargo did. He was their prisoner and might well be put to death, but at that moment, all that mattered was the luscious body being offered to him. Sinking to his knees between her legs, he pried at his belt buckle. His empty holster mocked him.

"Permit me." Sabina finished undoing his gun belt and tossed it from them. Her fingers found the top of his buckskin pants and peeled them down over his hips as she might peel a banana skin.

Not to be outdone, Fargo worked at the tiny buttons on her dress. There had to be twenty. When her dress parted, he had a chemise and then, to his annoyance, a corset to deal with. He lost his patience after a few minutes and said out loud, "To hell with it."

"What is wrong?" Sabina asked. She had been running her fingers through his hair and nibbling on his neck.

"Tell me you wear a chastity belt and we can forget this."

Sabina laughed loudly. Too loudly. Quickly covering her mouth with her hand, she said between bouts of giggling, "I have not been chaste since I was sixteen."

Fargo slid the hem of her dress up her willowy legs. She had near-ankle-length cotton drawers on underneath and he delved his hand up under them. Her skin had a satiny sheen that brought a lump of desire to his throat.

Sabina kissed his ear, his throat, his chin. She freed her breasts and cupped one, offering her nipple. Like a hawk swooping from on high, Fargo swooped to her mounds. He inhaled her nipple and nipped it lightly with his teeth.

"Oh, yes," Sabina breathed. Arching her back, she dug her nails into his shoulders.

Fargo had to slip his fingers up under the bottom of her corset to get at the tie to her drawers. But it would not come loose. He was about ready to rip it from her body when he felt it give, and a moment later he had slid her cotton drawers down and off.

"Took you long enough," Sabina teased.

It was the wrong thing to say. Gripping her hips, Fargo stopped with the foreplay. He touched the tip of his pole to her moist slit and then, in a single hard thrust, impaled her.

Sabina threw back her head. Her eyes were wide, her nostrils dilated. She stifled whatever outcry she was about to make, and suddenly sank her teeth into his shoulder, biting him.

Fargo didn't mind. Rough or gentle, it was all the same to him. He switched his mouth to her other breast while moving his hips back and in. Her body responded with rising ardor.

Vaguely, Fargo was aware that the Russians out at the

campfires were still singing and dancing. Inside the tent the only sounds were Sabina's heavy breathing and soft groans. With increasing urgency he rammed up into her, seeking to bring her to the brink.

Sabina clutched the blankets and arched her back. Her legs became a vise. It was a prelude to the wild ride that was to come as she gushed and gushed and gushed. Her release triggered Fargo's. Eventually the violence of their passion was spent and they coasted to a stop and lay gasping for breath and covered with sweat.

"You were magnificent," Sabina whispered. Her eyes were shut now, and she breathed more and more slowly.

Fargo rolled onto his side and lay waiting. It was not long before she succumbed to slumber. He wanted to sleep, too, but he had something more important to do, namely, save his skin. Easing off the blankets, he quickly dressed, strapped his gun belt back on, jammed his hat on his head, and quietly moved to the tent flap. Untying it, he peered out. The two men assigned to guard him were twenty feet away, their backs to the tent, watching the antics at the campfires.

Slipping out, Fargo closed the flap, then back-stepped around the tent, never taking his eyes off the guards until the tent was between him and them. Wheeling, he made for the horses.

A sentry had been posted, but this man, too, was staring toward the campfires. By his expression, he dearly yearned to be there.

Dropping flat, Fargo circled to come up on the man from behind. He had to move fast, faster than he liked, because he had no way of knowing how long Sabina would sleep. The smart thing was to slit her throat with the toothpick while she slept but there were lines he would not cross, and killing a defenseless woman was one of them.

The singing and dancing masked what slight sounds Fargo made. He was almost to his quarry when the man unexpectedly began to stretch, and turned. The man saw him at the same instant that Fargo drove his fist into the man's stomach. It bent the man in half. A second blow, to the back of the head, felled him.

Fargo had used his knuckles but it still hurt his hand. Shaking it, he relieved the sentry of a rifle and a revolver. The rifle was a single-shot Russian model, heavy and cumbersome. The ammo was in a pouch Fargo also helped himself to. The revolver, though, was British made, a Beaumont-Adams. Fargo had seen them now and again on the frontier. The grips were long and thin, the revolver itself shaped differently from a Colt. It was a bit unwieldy and felt alien in his hand. But beggars could not be choosers, as the saying went, and his own weapons were who knew where.

He dashed to the horse string. The bay was midway down. Drawing the toothpick from its ankle sheath, he cut the bay free. His saddle, saddle blanket, and bridle were with the rest, over near the campfires. He would be caught if he went for them, so he fashioned a hackamore from the rope.

About to swing up, Fargo glanced at the long line of horses, then toward the tents. The Russians would be after him in force as soon as they discovered he was missing. "How about if I slow them down?" he whispered to the bay.

Accordingly, Fargo drew the toothpick once more and set to work. He soon had the animals cut free. Weary from a day of hard riding, they did not run off, so he gave them incentive. Climbing on the bay, he whooped like a Comanche and fired into the air. That was all it took. To a horse, they whirled and bolted down the valley.

Cries of alarm brought a grin to Fargo's face. Yipping and hollering, he galloped after the horses. A few shots shattered the night but he was not overly worried. The dust the horses raised combined with the dark made it extremely unlikely anyone could fix a bead on him.

Fargo was pleased with himself. He regretted the loss of the Henry and the Colt but he could always buy new ones once he got back to the United States. It amused and amazed him that the Russians had not bothered to check under his buckskin shirt. They surely would have discovered the leather money belt with his poker winnings.

As for the gold, Fargo had two choices. He could go to the Russian authorities and lodge a formal protest. He could accuse Vassily Baranof of stealing the claim, but it suddenly dawned on him that Toomey and he had never gone to the claims office to have his name added. He had no proof he was half owner. Even if the Russians took his word, it could be months before an official investigation was completed and Vassily was charged with a crime. Months of twiddling his thumbs in Sitka, with no guarantee Vassily would be found guilty. The wily Russian was bound to use his considerable power and influence to escape the legal net, leaving Fargo with nothing to show for his ordeal.

Then there was Frank Toomey, trussed up fit for slaughter. Poor, naive Frank Toomey, who was too damn trusting for his own good. Frank Toomey, who had lost the claim fairly, and honored that loss where others might have tried to weasel out.

"Oh, hell," Fargo said, and came to a stop. He glanced back the way he had come. No Russians were in sight yet, but they were bound to trail their horses. Without mounts, their prospects for living were slim. The wilds of Alaska was no place to be stranded afoot.

Fargo wheeled the bay. With most of the men off after the horses, it should be easy to slip in, free Toomey, and slip out again. Maybe he could get his hands on the Henry and the Colt while he was at it.

He rode warily, listening intently. The usual bedlam reigned—the howls of wolves, the screech of a big cat, the occasional grunt of a roving bear. To the south an owl hooted. Another owl answered to the north. He went a little farther and a third owl hooted to the west.

Again Fargo stopped. His hand strayed to the Beaumont-Adams, wedged under his belt near the buckle. Every nerve in his body tingled. His senses straining into the night, he angled to the right toward cover.

Suddenly the bay pricked its ears and snorted. It was staring at the trees Fargo was riding toward. He changed direction, making for the end of the valley and the Russian camp.

To the left of Fargo, something moved, something quick and low to the ground. Those who did not know better might mistake it for a coyote or some other animal. But Fargo did know better. He had been on the frontier too long to be deceived.

Swinging toward it, Fargo drew the Beaumont-Adams. But even as he shifted in the saddle he realized he had blundered and fallen for one of the oldest tricks around.

Fargo started to swing back toward the trees but it was too late. Much too late. He heard the patter of onrushing footfalls barely a heartbeat before a heavy form slammed into him.

13

Fargo's agility served him well. He twisted as he fell, his hand locked on a throat, and turned his attacker so that his attacker struck the ground first and he landed on top of him, his knee gouging deep into an unprotected stomach. A whoosh of breath and an outcry testified to the pain he had inflicted. Leaping clear, he leveled the Russian rifle. Or tried to.

They swarmed him. They came out of the dark in a wave and swamped him with their numbers. The rifle was torn from his grasp. The Beaumont-Adams was wrested from under his belt. He fought them as best he was able but he was one man and there had to be ten or more, and the outcome was never in doubt. That they did not kill him surprised him and worried him more than a little.

His arms held fast, Fargo was hauled to his feet. Rough hands seized the back of his shirt and he was propelled into the pines. He did not resist. His attackers were not Russian. The smell of them, and the way they moved and fought, had told them who they were.

Indians.

The pines thinned. Eventually the ground sloped into a hollow. It was there they had their camp. A single fire, kept small the Indian way. Twenty more warriors were hunkered in patient Indian fashion. All of them rose.

One, older than the rest, came forward. He had the wrinkles of many years, more years than most men, red or white, ever saw.

Fargo was flung to his knees. They did not strike him or restrain him. There was no need. Over thirty warriors ringed him. He was at their mercy. He knew it, and they knew he knew it.

Their weapons were the first thing Fargo noticed. None had guns. A few had bows. Others held short stabbing spears. All had knives, unusual knives, in that each knife had a long stabbing blade at one end and a short blade at the other end, with a grip in the middle.

Next Fargo studied the men. His captors were short of stature. They were not stocky, not in the way some Apaches were stocky, but they were powerfully built, with wide chests and broad shoulders. Their faces were swarthy ovals, with long, thin noses and square chins. Their dark hair was cut short and trimmed around the ears. Some had mustaches, unusual for Indians south of Canada but not unusual here in the northland. All the men had nose rings. Quite a few wore headbands of leather. Hide tunics and leggings were the preferred attire. Not crude tunics, either, but finely made, with painted figures and symbols. Many a face was painted, as well.

The old man rested his hand on his double-bladed knife and regarded Fargo with interest. He said something in Russian.

"I don't savvy the tongue," Fargo said.

With a grunt, the old warrior switched to English. "Your kind call me Gray Fox."

"You're the one who showed Frank Toomey where to find the gold," Fargo remembered. "You are a Tlingit, if I recollect rightly."

Gray Fox smiled a sly smile. "That was me, yes. Like all your kind, he was so greedy he did not think to wonder why I would do such a thing."

"I have wondered," Fargo said. "Gold is valuable to the red man as well as to the white."

"My people have little use for it," Gray Fox said. "But to you and your kind it is everything."

"There you go again," Fargo said. "What do you mean by my kind?"

"White men."

"Not all whites are the same, just as not all Indians are the same," Fargo mentioned.

"So you say," Gray Fox skeptically replied. He looked up as the bay was brought close to the fire, then listened to a recital by one of the warriors who had helped capture Fargo. Whatever the warrior told him produced a puzzled expression. "You ran off the horses of your brother Bear Men?"

"The who?"

"Your people, the Russians. To us you are big and hairy like bears, so we call you Bear Men."

"I am American, not Russian."

"You are white," Gray Fox said.

"I just told you. Not all white men are alike. I do not come from Russia. I come from another country," Fargo stressed. He sensed it was important. He could tell by the old warrior's tone that Russians were not his favorite people.

"To us there is no difference."

"Are the Tlingits the same as the Haida? Are they the same as the Eyak or the Bellacoola?"

Gray Fox was slow in answering. "No, they are not."

"Even so, Americans and Russians are different people. Russian ways are not our ways. Many Americans are in Alaska but it is not our land. It belongs to the Russians."

Gray Fox's swarthy features clouded. "It belongs to my people. It belongs to the other tribes who were here before the Bear People came. It has been ours for as far back as my people can remember."

"I am not one of the Bear People," Fargo reiterated, but the old warrior did not seem to hear him.

"Before their kind came, the Tlingits were happy. We fished. We hunted. Our enemies were few, our villages were safe. We prospered." Gray Fox was gazing into the past, not at Fargo. "Then those you call Russians arrived, in boats as big as houses. At first they were friendly. They smiled a lot, and traded many fine and wonderful things for our furs. We thought it splendid of them."

Fargo said nothing. He had seen it happen elsewhere. The pattern was always the same and always ended as Gray Fox's account would end.

"But then more of them came. They did not go back on the boats as the others had, but built houses of their own on land that was not theirs to build on. We said to them, 'You cannot stay.' But they laughed at us, and told us they would do as they pleased and, worse, *we* were to do as they pleased. They wanted us to do as they would have us do. We were to be their slaves, whether we wanted to be or not."

"I have heard the story," Fargo said.

"My people refused. The elders of my people and those of the Aleuts tried to reason with them but they would not listen. Their ears were closed to us. So we rose up against them. We killed the Bear People and burned Sitka, and we thought that would be the end of it." Gray Fox stopped.

"But it wasn't."

"No, it was not," Gray Fox said sadly. "More boats came, and more Russians. They rebuilt their town. Now it is bigger than ever, and many men with guns keep us from burning it down a second time."

"There are too many soldiers," Fargo acknowledged.

"They still trade with us," Gray Fox said. "They still want our furs. So they act as if nothing ever happened. As if we did not burn them out and drive them off. Yet we see the hate in their eyes and in their hearts, and we are not fooled."

"What does all that have to do with why you are here in this valley?" Fargo wanted to know.

The ancient Tlingit grew sadder still. "I have seen many winters. I was one of those who helped burn Sitka. I hated the Bear People. They had killed my son. My only son. I still hate them. They think the Tlingits have forgotten but we have not. They think we are content to go on pretending they are our friends, but we know who our enemies are."

"I am not your enemy," Fargo said.

Gray Fox blinked and looked at him. "You are white. Yesterday I would have said that is enough to have you killed. But if you speak true, I must think some more."

"What do you plan for the other whites?"

"They are Russian, are they not?"

"All but two," Fargo said. "They are Americans like me."

"Yes. Toomey, the one I brought to see the gold. And the white with the belly and the chins." Gray Fox paused. "We have been watching you since you left Sitka."

"Speaking of Toomey," Fargo interjected, "why *did* you bring him here? If you hate whites so much, why help one find that which whites value most?"

"I took him for one of the Bear People," Gray Fox said. "I had heard he hunted the yellow metal so I went to him and told him I knew where some could be found."

"Why haven't the Tlingits dug out the gold for themselves?" Fargo wondered.

"And have the whites take it from us and leave us nothing?" Gray Fox rejoined.

"I still don't get what you are up to," Fargo said. Although, the truth be known, he had more than an inkling.

"When one white finds yellow ore, many whites follow," Gray Fox said. "Greed brings them. As greed brought these others. Now there are that many more to kill."

Fargo absorbed that. "You wanted more whites to come. The gold was bait."

"The gold was bait," Gray Fox admitted.

"You intend to wipe them out?"

"Not one will leave this valley alive. I will have my revenge for my son." Gray Fox shook with intense emotion as he said it.

"But that was decades ago," Fargo said. "Why have you waited so long to get back at them?"

"So I can kill the one who leads them."

"Vassily Baranof?" Fargo tried to make sense of that. "How does he fit in?"

"His name. Baranof. It was a Baranof who made slaves of the Aleuts those many winters ago. It was that Baranof who tried to make slaves of the Tlingits." Gray Fox paused. "It was that Baranof who shot my son."

Fargo had it then. "After all these years, you aim to make the Baranof family pay for killing your boy by killing Vassily. Blood for blood. Is that how it goes?"

"One of my family for one of theirs."

"But that still doesn't tell me why you waited so long," Fargo pointed out. "Why didn't you kill the Baranof who squeezed the trigger?"

"I wanted to," Gray Fox admitted. "I wanted to more than I have ever wanted anything. But he was protected. I could not get close. Later he left. His son came for a while but I could not get close to the son, either. Then, four months ago as you whites measure time, I learned of this new Baranof. I learned he loves money. It came to me that here was my chance."

Fargo had to marvel at the depth of the old warrior's hate. It made him think of the hill clans of the deep South, where blood feuds were waged for generations. It was another reminder, as if any were needed, that in some respects the white man and the red man were a lot more alike than either was willing to admit.

"But I was clever," Gray Fox had gone on. "I did not try to strike at him directly. I led the other one, Toomey, to the gold. I knew Baranof would hear of it, and when he came, I would follow him." He stopped and looked at Fargo as if to say, *Do you understand now?*

Fargo had to hand it to him. Odds were, no matter when or how Vassily heard about the gold, he was bound to investigate. So that part of Gray Fox's plan had worked. "Weren't you worried when Toomey left for Seattle?"

"No. He told me why he was going, and that he would be back. All I had to do was wait. As you say, I have been patient for years. What were a few more weeks or months?"

"And you kept watch on Vassily. So when he left Sitka, you could follow him."

"Me or my friends," Gray Fox said, and gestured at the ring of Tlingit warriors.

So there it was. Fargo's high hand in a poker game had cast him smack into the middle of a vendetta involving Russians and Indians the Russians had clashed with sixty years ago. "Sometimes life is too damn ridiculous for words," Fargo said.

Gray Fox leaped to the wrong conclusion. "Ridiculous? That means silly. Was the death of my son silly? Was it silly of the Bear People to make slaves of the tribes that had lived here since the dawn of forever?"

"That is not what I meant," Fargo said, quickly adding, "You speak good English for someone who hates whites so much."

"I speak eight tongues," Gray Fox stated. "We Indians are not as stupid as many of you whites think we are."

"I'm not one of them."

"I would like to believe you," Gray Fox said. "Your eyes do not hold contempt for me. They do not hold hate. If more whites were like you, there would not be so much killing."

"Frank Toomey is like me," Fargo stretched the truth. "He does not hate Indians, either."

"He does not hate us," Gray Fox conceded, "but he thinks we are slow and primitive. His very words to me one night." The old warrior chuckled. "He tried to get me to give up my heathen ways and accept his white god as the one true god."

"He does not know any better," Fargo defended him.

"He does not know much at all," Gray Fox said. "But you are right. It is not him I hate. We will spare him if we can. Him, and the one with the belly and the chins."

"Which brings us back to me."

"Yes. It does." Gray Fox absently fondled his knife. "I will sleep on what to do with you. Until then you will sit by the fire. I will not have you tied but do not try to run. My friends would stop you, and some of them have a saying they are fond of. You would find it most interesting."

"Care to tell me what it is?"

"More of my kind should live by it." Gray Fox grinned. "The only good white is a dead white."

14

Skye Fargo faced a dilemma. There was a chance Gray Fox would convince the other Tlingits to let him go. If he sat there quietly until morning, they might let him take the bay and ride off down the valley. But come the morning something else was going to happen. The Tlingits intended to massacre the Russians. Toomey might be spared, or he might not.

Then there were the women. Fargo did not give a lick what happened to Vassily and the rest of his crew. But the women were another matter. The simple fact that they were female brought out in him the protective impulse it would bring out in most any male.

The interlude in Sabina's tent did not persuade him one way or the other. She had bedded him, not the other way around. To her, he was a plaything, a dalliance she could discard once she had her way with him.

But Sabina was female, and Kira was female, and that made all the difference. Fargo could not let them be slaughtered. Nor did the notion of what the warriors would do with them before the warriors killed them sit well with him. He was not a red-hater. It was just that there were some things that were not done, or should not be done, by red or white. Raping women was one of them. He would no more stand still for red men raping white women any more than he would stand still for white men raping red women.

So it was that Fargo sat quietly as if he had been cowed by Gray Fox's threat, but the whole time he watched the Tlingits from under his hat brim. Watched and waited.

The warriors held a counsel. Afterward, six of their number headed into the forest while the rest lay down to rest. They had no blankets. They curled up where they were and went to sleep, their weapons close at hand.

Gray Fox came over to Fargo. "Are you scared, white man?" The prospect seemed to please him.

"Where did the others go?"

"To watch the Russians, who are searching for their horses. But they will not find them. Some of us caught the horses you ran off and are bringing them here." That, too, pleased the old warrior. "You have done us a great favor, American."

"I did?"

"We planned to run off the horses ourselves. You saved us the trouble." Gray Fox grinned. "On foot the Russians cannot escape. They do not know it yet but they are trapped. We can do with them as we want." He stopped and raised his gaze to the stars. "Tomorrow, after all these winters, my son will be avenged."

"Will you sleep better then?" Fargo asked.

"Yes."

"I had no idea the Tlingits were so bloodthirsty."

"We do not kill just to kill. We do not make war just to make war," Gray Fox said. "But we fight when we have to and we go to war when we have to. Tomorrow we have to."

Fargo swept a hand toward the other Tlingits. "Do all of them want to kill the Russians because of your son?"

"Oh, no," Gray Fox said. "But they have grandfathers or fathers or cousins or friends who have suffered at Russian hands." He swept his own hand as Fargo had. "All of them, like me, want revenge. All of them, like me, will be satisfied with nothing less than blood."

Fargo had to try, so he asked, "Is there any chance I can convince you to spare the women?"

"No."

"They are females."

"The Russians have treated our females and females of other tribes in ways that make me hot with anger."

"You like sayings. There is one in my country. Two wrongs do not make a right."

Gray Fox grew thoughtful. "Interesting. So if someone is wronged, they should not seek vengeance?"

"That is the idea, yes."

"It is a stupid idea, fit only for the weak and the timid. A man must have his revenge when he is wronged or he is not much of a man." Gray Fox's eyes narrowed. "Tell me. Are you one of those whites who carry a big book around? If someone walks up to you and hits you in the face, do you turn your face so they can hit you again?"

"If someone hits me, I hit them harder," Fargo answered honestly.

Gray Fox laughed. "You think like a Tlingit. In the morning my people will hit hard at those who have hurt us." He turned and went off to talk to another warrior. Shortly thereafter, he eased to the ground, and with his hands for a pillow, he was soon asleep.

Fargo lay down, too, but he only pretended to sleep. He saw that only two sentries had been posted, one on the north rim of the hollow and the other on the south rim. That made it easier for him.

Unfortunately, he could not take the bay. The Tlingits had produced a rope and tied it to a stake. Warriors slept quite close to it, some so close it was a wonder the bay did not step on them.

Having made up his mind, Fargo inched his fingers into his boot and palmed the Arkansas toothpick. Half an hour went by. An hour. By then he was convinced that every Tlingit except for the sentries was asleep.

Easing onto his stomach, Fargo slowly pushed into a crouch. He was closer to the west rim than the east rim so he crept west, threading through the sleeping figures with extreme care. Some of the warriors were snoring.

Others muttered or smacked their lips as if eating something, or made other noises. He watched their eyes, always their eyes, for any telltale hint that they were about to wake up. His skin constantly prickled, as if from a heat rash, and several times he narrowly avoided being touched when a sleeping figure unexpectedly rolled over and flung out an arm or a leg.

He also had to keep an eye on the sentries. Both were intent on the surrounding woods and only rarely glanced into the hollow. When they did, he instantly froze.

Fargo skirted a warrior who had thrust out an arm that nearly brushed his leg. Cautiously stepping over it, he looked up to find the sentry on the north rim peering down at the sleepers. He flattened, hoping he had not been seen.

The sentry raised a hand to his mouth as if to shout an alarm, and Fargo tensed, preparing to bolt. But the sentry only rubbed his chin and then turned toward the forest.

Ten more minutes it took. Ten minutes for Fargo to reach the west rim and crawl up out of the hollow. Once he was in among the spruce, he rose and ran, circling wide so the sentries would not hear him. When he was sure he was out of earshot, he ran flat out for the Russian camp. He had miles to cover. It would take hours. But he should get there well before dawn and would warn Vassily so Vassily could protect the women. That, and somehow get Frank Toomey out.

Preoccupied with thoughts of the Russians and the Tlingits, Fargo belatedly realized something was shadowing him. He distinctly heard the crackle and snap of underbrush. Suddenly stopping, he listened. Whatever was out there also stopped.

Fargo's mouth went dry. Judging by the sound it might be a bear, and if it was, he stood no chance in hell, not when all he had was the toothpick. The next moment the thing grunted, and there could be no doubt. It *was* a bear, and it was stalking him.

Fargo thought of another saying. When it rains, it pours. He glanced about and selected a nearby spruce.

Darting over, he began to climb. None too soon. With a tremendous crash of rending limbs and torn vegetation, an enormous bulk hurtled out of the night toward him. He was barely ten feet off the ground when the bear struck the trunk with an impact that nearly sent Fargo plummeting. Spurred by the image of four- to five-inch claws shredding his body, Fargo clambered another ten feet, then looked down.

His nocturnal stalker rose onto two legs. The thing was gigantic. Another Alaskan brown bear, and this one was hungry.

"If I didn't have bad luck I wouldn't have any luck at all," Fargo muttered.

The bear let out with a roar that silenced the entire valley. From end to end, the wolves and coyotes and night birds and other animals fell quiet as the ferocious challenge echoed off the mountain slopes and was borne on the wind.

Enough starlight filtered through the canopy for Fargo to see a pair of baleful eyes staring up at him. The eyes seemed to glow with inner fire. The brown bear reached up a giant paw and swiped at the tree, its claws raking furrows in the bark.

Fargo was safe enough. The bear was too heavy to climb, and the tree was too big for the bear to push over. But every minute the bear kept him there was a minute less he had to reach the Russians and warn them about the Tlingits. Breaking off part of a branch, he threw it at the bear's face, saying, "Shoo! Scat! Go pester someone else, you hairy bastard."

Another roar, louder than the first, shook the very air, and the bear tried unsuccessfully to scale the trunk. Its massive weight caused two limbs to break and it gave up. It was content to stand and glare.

Fargo looked at the toothpick in his hand and laughed. A knife was a poor substitute for a gun. Only a heavy-caliber weapon could drop a monster like the one below. Arrows could not do it. Spears could not do it. A slug to the brain pan, the heart, or the lungs was the only sure method, and even then the bear's indomitable will and unrivaled stamina might keep it alive long enough to slay its slayer.

Fargo made himself as comfortable as he could. The bear had begun pacing, circling the tree. It plainly was not inclined to go after easier prey.

That worried him. Fargo had heard tales of men treed for hours, even days, by bears that would not relent. He did not have hours, let alone days, to spare. He must get to the Russian camp before dawn or a lot of people were going to lose their lives, among them Sabina and Kira.

Time dragged. The brown bear paced and paced and paced some more, as tireless as a steam engine. Every now and again it would look up at Fargo and growl.

Fargo had to do something but he was at a loss as to what. He could swing down and run for it but he would not get ten yards before the bear overtook him.

Then the wind shifted. The brown bear stopped pacing and raised its muzzle. Sniffing loudly, it moved toward a thicket. A startled yelp burst from the thicket's depths, and a second later so did a two-legged form in a tunic and leather headband, fleeing as if the hounds of hell were after it. Only in this instance, it was something worse.

Voicing another roar, the brown bear gave chase.

Fargo did not linger to see the outcome. Swiftly descending, he struck off for the valley's end. He stayed alert for other Tlingits but did not see any. After much hard travel fraught with the uncertainty of not knowing if the brown bear would come after him, or some other predator might pick up his scent, he spied fingers of flame dancing in the dark ahead and slowed.

Now that he was almost to the camp, Fargo had another problem. He would not put it past Vassily's underlings to shoot him on sight. Somehow he must get to Vassily himself, or the women. Sabina would keep him alive long enough for him to warn them. Then it was in their hands.

Fargo bore to the right. If he remembered correctly,

Vassily's tent was near the trees on that side. With a little luck, if no guards were near, he could slip in without being shot at.

The camp was as still as a cemetery. It occurred to Fargo that most of the men, Vassily included, must be out searching for the horses. He came to the edge of the trees. So far he had not spied a single soul, but Vassily would not go off and leave the camp unprotected.

The fires still blazed, so someone had to be tending them. Fargo scoured the shadows. He scanned the tents. Nothing moved, and there were no sounds, not even snoring.

Puzzled, Fargo glided into the open. He had the toothpick in his hand but it would be next to useless against a rifle or a revolver. He cat-footed to Vassily's tent. The flap was closed but it was not tied. Opening it, he peered in.

Vassily was not there.

Growing more perplexed by the moment, Fargo moved to the next tent, and the one after that. No one, anywhere. He stopped and was debating whether to give a holler when muffled sounds from over near the aspens caught his attention. Warily venturing closer, he saw someone on the ground among the trees. Someone bound hand and foot and gagged.

Hastening over, Fargo knelt. "I'll have you free in no time," he whispered, and carefully cut the rope looped around Frank Toomey's ankles.

Toomey was frantically trying to say something. A sock had been stuffed in his mouth and secured in place with a piece of rope.

"Hold on," Fargo said, and pried at the knots. It took some doing but presently they parted.

Toomey promptly yanked the sock from his mouth and commenced spitting and coughing. "Dear God, that was awful! The stink! It about made me gag."

"Hush up or they'll hear you," Fargo warned.

Still coughing and spitting, Toomey shook his head. "I think they all left. They went after the horses."

"They left you unguarded? Left the tents and all their belongings?"

"They were in a panic," Toomey said. "You should have seen them. Without their horses they are in trouble." He smiled. "Darned clever of you." Toomey held out his wrists for Fargo to cut the rope. "Now we can get out of here."

"Have you seen any sign of the Tlingits?" Fargo asked.

"Tlingits? What would they be doing here?" Toomey gazed anxiously about. "This is getting more—" He abruptly stopped, his eyes widening in stark fear.

Fargo whirled. He thought it would be Russians or maybe Tlingits but he was wrong.

Something stood amid the tents. Something as big as the tents themselves.

"Dear God!" Toomey breathed.

It was the brown bear.

15

In the flickering glow of the campfires, the brown bear truly had the aspect of a monster. Immense beyond measure, it embodied every fear the human heart harbored, every dread the human mind could conceive. It was so huge and so fearsome that it was not uncommon for its prey to freeze in sheer fright.

Fargo froze, but for a different reason. Bears were drawn to movement and he did not want the bear to charge them. It was sniffing at a tent. Or so Fargo thought until a burly Russian leaped up and looked confusedly about him, a rifle in his hands. The guard Vassily had posted had fallen asleep. No doubt he had lain down close to the tent so no one could see him. His back was to the brown bear and he did not realize it was behind him until it growled.

The Russian turned and bleated in horror. He was nose to nose with the largest carnivore on the continent and he did what most would do. His nerve broke and he turned and fled. Or tried to, for he had hardly taken three strides when the brown bear was on him, smashing him to earth with an almost casual swat of an enormous paw.

The Russian screamed. From his shoulders to his waist, his back had been ripped to ribbons by the bear's raking claws. His coat and shirt were in tatters. So was his flesh.

Incredibly, his spine was visible, the white of the bone a pale contrast to the rich scarlet of the blood pumping from the wounds.

The man did not give up. Frantic, he crawled toward a tent, but again he had gone only a few yards when the brown bear brought the same paw that had raked his back smashing down on it, pinning the man to the ground. Shrieking, the Russian struggled to wriggle out from under but the brown bear held him down as effortlessly as Fargo might hold a fly.

Twisting his head, the guard looked up into the descending maw of death. He screamed. The crunch of his skull as the brown bear's jaws closed was frighteningly loud.

Frank Toomey whined like a stricken puppy. He started to stand but Fargo grabbed his wrist and whispered, "Stay right where you are."

The brown bear was shaking its victim as a terrier might shake a rat.

"Let go of me!" Toomey mewed, tugging to be free.

"Don't move," Fargo warned.

"We have to hide before it sees us!" Toomey insisted. Again he tried to pull loose but Fargo would not let go.

"Stay still, damn it." Fargo had not taken his eyes off the brown bear. It had torn the Russian's head from his body and was gnawing at the top of the head, apparently in an effort to get at the brains.

Toomey did not know when he was well off. "I said let go!" he yelled, and jerked backward.

There was only so much stupidity Fargo would abide. He let go, diving into the aspens as he did.

The brown bear had dropped the head and was staring fixedly at Toomey in the manner bears had before they attacked.

Seconds ago Frank Toomey had been set to flee. But now, paralyzed with fear, he blurted, "No, no. Dear God in heaven, please."

The brown bear grunted.

Toomey ran. But in his abject fear he did not run into the aspens, as he should have. He ran toward the nearest slope. He was not thinking, for even if he reached it, it offered no cover, no haven from the beast pursuing him. And the brown bear was after him, although at a leisurely pace, almost as if the bear knew Toomey could not get away and it was not going to exert itself more than it had to.

"No!" Toomey reached the slope and raced up it, but in his haste and excitement, he slipped. He came down hard on his hands and knees, screeched in terror, and made it halfway to his feet.

The brown bear's paw flashed once, twice, three times, and what was left of Frank Toomey crumpled in a mangled heap. The bear pawed at the body, then ponderously turned and gazed into the aspens.

A chill spiked through Fargo. The bear had seen him. It was looking for him, looking to do what it had done to Toomey and the guard. Panic welled, and it was all Fargo could do to keep from making the same mistake Toomey had made.

But Fargo had encountered bears before. Maybe not Alaskan brown bears, maybe not bears bigger than buffalo, but he had run into large black bears and even larger grizzlies, and he had learned not to give in to fear.

One of Toomey's legs was convulsing. The brown bear looked down at it, then nipped at the knee. Its teeth sheared clean through. A crimson geyser spurted, and like a cub frolicking in the watery spray of a river, the brown bear held its great head under the red spray and let the blood splash over it.

Fargo began to crawl backward. If he could slip off while the brown bear feasted, he could yet save his hide. But no sooner did he start than movement in the camp caused him to stop.

A tent flap had opened. The flap to the tent the women used. A head poked out, a lovely head crowned with dark hair. Sabina glanced both ways, then beckoned to someone behind her. She stepped out, Kira at her heels.

Fargo opened his mouth to shout. But if he did the bear might come after him. For a span of heartbeats he hesitated, trying to think of a better way. But there was none. Especially since the women, unaware of the brown bear on the slope, were moving into the open where the bear would see them.

"Sabina! Kira! Run off down the valley!" Fargo shouted, and darted from the aspens. The brown bear's head had snapped up at his shout and the bear was staring fixedly at him.

"Chase me, bear! Me!" Fargo yelled, and turned to run back into the trees.

Too late, Fargo saw that Sabina and Kira had not run off as he had told them, but were running toward him. "No!" he bellowed. "Go back! The bear will see you!"

"What bear?" Sabina asked as she stepped past the last of the tents. She spotted it then and turned to stone, but the harm had been done. The bear had spotted her.

For all of a minute, the tableau did not change—Fargo, by the aspens, armed with only his toothpick; Sabina, by the tents, her hand pressed to her throat in shock; Kira, behind the last tent, too scared to move or cry out; and the Alaskan brown bear, spattered with the blood and gore from two victims.

Then Sabina screamed and bolted, not back in among the tents but toward the slope on the far side. If she thought she could outrun the brown bear, she was mistaken. A grown bear could overtake and bring down a horse.

Fargo hoped the brown bear would let her go. By rights it should have been content with Toomey and the guard. But bears were notorious for being unpredictable, and this bear was no exception.

Sabina's next scream rose to the stars. The brown bear was after her, moving with astounding swiftness for something so big.

Firming his grip on the toothpick, Fargo rushed to intercept it. He was closer to Sabina and he figured to block its path and hold it at bay long enough for her to hide. But even he reckoned without the bear's speed. It pounded past without so much as a glance in his direction.

"Lie down and don't move!" Fargo hollered. He had heard that worked sometimes—that a bear would sniff and paw but leave the person alone.

Sabina heard. She was almost to the slope but she stopped dead and dropped, curling into a ball with her arms over her head and face. She was whimpering and trembling.

The brown bear reached her. It cocked its head from side to side, and then bit her arm and with a powerful wrench, tore her arm off.

Fargo stopped. There was nothing he could do. Not now. Not with blood spurting by the gallon from the stump. She did not scream much; she passed out before the end came.

Scarcely breathing, Fargo sidestepped toward the tents. The bear had temporarily forgotten about him and was tearing at her abdomen in a feeding frenzy.

Kira was cowering in fright. She was riveted to the ghastly spectacle of her best friend being devoured, and jumped when Fargo touched her arm. She opened her mouth to say something and Fargo instantly clamped a hand over it and whispered in her ear, "Not a sound. Back away slowly. We are getting the hell out of here."

They started to do just that. Then, to Fargo's consternation, Kira stopped and pointed at Vassily's tent. Without explaining why, she moved toward it, her eyes never leaving the brown bear.

"What are you doing?" Fargo whispered. They had no time for this. The bear would be done eating soon and might decide to poke around in the tents or to destroy them. Bears loved to disport themselves at campsites, leaving ruin in their wake.

"Come," Kira whispered, motioning. "You will like much lots."

"Like what?" Fargo whispered, his anger rising when she did not answer. He had half a mind to throw her over his shoulder and carry her off. He overtook her just as she came to the tent and opened the flap. "Stop." He snatched at her wrist but did not get a good grip and she twisted loose and darted in. Downright mad, he went in after her. "What the hell do you think you are doing?" he demanded.

"I see him do."

"Saw who do what?"

She was referring to a long wicker basket. Apparently it contained some of Vassily's personal effects. Unfastening the clasp on the lid, she opened it and pointed. "We these need, yes?"

Fargo went over. He thought she was after food or some such. One look, and he wanted to kiss her. Lying on top of clothes and other articles were his Colt and his Henry and his spare box of ammo for the rifle.

"I see Vassily do," Kira said in her imperfect English. "Sabina and me here." At mention of her friend, her eyes misted. She was on the verge of tears.

Fargo hugged her. It was the best he could do under the circumstances. "Hold it in," he whispered. "There will be plenty of time to cry after we put a lot of miles between us and that damn bear."

"Shoot damn bear," Kira urged. "Kill with gun."

So that was why she brought him to get them, Fargo realized. He scooped up the Colt and checked that it was loaded, saying, "It takes a cannon to drop a bear that size. I need a heavier caliber rifle."

"Can kill with pretty long gun," Kira said, smacking the Henry's brass receiver as he raised it.

"It might not bring him down," Fargo said. "We can't risk it."

Kira stamped her small foot and snapped much too loudly, "Kill it! Kill for Sabina!"

Fargo was making sure the Henry was loaded. "We tangle with that bear, we might be the losers." He crammed the box of ammunition in a pocket.

"I want big bear dead!" Kira insisted, stamping her foot again.

Fargo seized her by the wrist and hauled her toward the flap. He swore when she dug in her heels and tried to twist loose. "Stop it, damn it."

"Kill bear!"

She practically shouted that last, and Fargo came close

to slugging her. He got her to the flap and shoved it aside, and they both stopped cold in their tracks. Fargo seldom experienced fear but he experienced it now.

Kira whimpered and cringed.

The brown bear was ten yards away, staring. It had heard them. Its maw was caked with bright fresh blood, and a strip of pink skin dangled from its lower jaw.

"Don't move a muscle," Fargo whispered. It was their only hope; that the bear had eaten enough and was not all that interested in them and would go off to sleep or whatever bears did when they had gorged themselves.

Kira was shaking.

Fargo could not blame her. He had his own fear under control or he might quake, too. The bear was so immense and they were so puny. If it charged, his days of wandering were over.

The next moment, to Fargo's amazement and profound relief, the brown bear did exactly as he wanted it to do. It wheeled and lumbered off with that peculiar gait all bears had. It did not look back but crossed to the aspens and disappeared.

Just like that, Kira was in his arms. She clung to him, weak with emotion, her warm hands on his neck. "It be gone! We is safe!"

"Luck," Fargo said. "Pure dumb luck." But he would take all the luck life threw at him.

"I much happy," Kira said. "We celerybrate."

"Celerybrate?" Fargo repeated, and laughed. "No. We still have to light a shuck."

Kira had gone to a corner where packs were haphazardly piled. She rummaged through them until she found the one she wanted. Opening it, she held up a bottle of vodka. She giggled as she brought it over and offered it to him. "We drink, eh?"

"Not now," Fargo said. He had other worries besides the bear. There were the Russians to think of, and the Tlingits. Either might show up at any moment. "Bring it with us if you want."

"No. Now." Kira said.

Fargo was losing his patience with her. She had nearly

gotten them mauled to death by fighting him when he wanted to leave, and now this. "We are still not safe. There are Indians out to slit our throats."

"What Indians? I no see Indians."

"Tlingits," Fargo said. "And I am not going to stand here and try to convince you. Either come with me or stay. Your choice. But I am leaving." He turned to the flap.

Kira gripped his hand. "I sorry. I not want mad make you. I come. I like you. I like big much."

"That's nice." Fargo was reaching for the flap when the blunder he had made hit him like a physical blow. His gut tightened and his head reeled. The brown bear had gone into the aspens—but there was nothing past the aspens except the hole with the gold vein and the rock cliff. There was no way out of the valley at that end.

"Why you do stop?" Kira asked.

Fargo did not answer. He opened the flap and the blood in his veins became ice.

The brown bear had come back.

16

In the instant Fargo beheld the bear he knew it was going to charge. Nothing the bear did told him, nothing in the way it held its body, nor did it growl nor snarl nor roar. Fargo just knew.

And it did.

Pushing Kira back, Fargo whipped the Henry to his shoulder. He had already levered a round into the chamber. In the blink of an eye he had sighted and thumbed back the hammer and fired. He aimed for the head, for the bear's right eye. The skull was too thick, the body a mass of muscle and bone only the heaviest slugs could penetrate, and from head-on he did not have a lung shot, anyway, so he went for the head, he went for the eye. He fired three times as fast as he could work the lever and put three slugs into the brown bear at a range of twenty yards. It had no more effect than if he had used a pea shooter.

The bear roared.

Standing stock-still so the rifle was as steady, Fargo sent three more slugs into the beast in the time it took the bear to cover fifteen feet and still the bear came hurtling on, impervious, indestructible.

The grim specter of death breathing down his neck, Fargo fired again and again and yet again, and *still* the bear came on.

Fargo had used nine of the fifteen rounds in the Henry. Six cartridges left and the bear was only ten yards away and closing fast. Ten yards, and Fargo would be ripped to bits as the guard and Sabina Baranof had been.

Strangely, Fargo's fear was gone. He felt only the baffled frustration any marksman would feel on putting nine shots into something and having that something not go down. And Fargo was a marksman. He had taken part in shooting contests where the best in the country competed for money, and he was rated among them.

As the brown bear came barreling on, Fargo aimed at that right eye and fired and worked the lever and aimed and fired and worked the lever again and aimed and fired and finally, finally, the brown bear broke stride. It stumbled and nearly fell, and Fargo worked the lever and sent another slug into the eye, and by now the bear was close enough that he could see the eye was gone; there was a hole where the eye had been.

The bear was almost on him. It was moving slowly, molasses could move faster, but it was almost on top of him, and Fargo fired and the bear crashed down inches from his legs and he thrust the Henry's muzzle into the hole where the eye had been and fired the last round.

In the sudden silence, Fargo's ears still thundered with the boom of his shots. He could hear his blood roar, hear the hammer of his heart. His whole body tingled, and when he sucked in a breath it was the sweetest breath he ever took.

A hand timidly touched Fargo's shoulder. Swallowing, he resisted an impulse to jump out of his boots.

"Big bear be dead?" Kira asked.

Fargo had to cough twice before he found his voice. "They don't get any deader."

"You kill it."

"You got what you wanted," Fargo said.

"You really kill it."

"I'd as soon not have had to." Fargo had come as close as he ever had to becoming worm food and he was still shaken.

Kira laughed and came around in front of him, nearly

tripping over the brown bear. Embracing him, she kissed him on the cheek. "We make revenge for Sabina. I thank you."

Fargo did not share her elation. When the brown bear attacked Sabina it was only doing what bears did. Bears ate things. Living things, sometimes. Bears did not distinguish between other prey and humans. To them, flesh was flesh. "We have to get out of here." He began reloading.

"Why get when bear be dead."

"Which is how Vassily wants me," Fargo reminded her. "Gather up whatever you want to take, but hurry."

"Vassily not want me dead," Kira said. "Vassily my people. I stay. They come back later or sooner."

"You can't stay here alone," Fargo said. "Those Indians I told you about won't care that you are a woman."

"I see no Indians. You sure?"

Fargo did not like being called a liar. "The Tlingits are out to slaughter your entire party. Stick with me and I will do my best to keep you alive."

"But Vassily—" Kira began.

"I will take you to him, if that's what you want," Fargo said. Then he would find a horse and light out for Sitka. Let the Russians and the Tlingits kill each other off. He wanted no part of it.

"Maybe so I be more safe here," Kira said.

Fargo tried one last time. "Have you been listening? The Indians will kill you if they find you."

"I hide," Kira said. "They not find. Vassily come, and all be well."

Fargo sighed. He never hit women unless they were trying to harm him, but he had a strong urge to try and smack some sense into her. "Everything dies," he said.

Kira blinked her lovely eyes. "I sorry?"

Nodding at the brown bear, Fargo repeated, "Everything dies. A bear as big as a log cabin. You. Me. Everything."

"Ah. You concern for me?" Kira kissed him on the other cheek. "You be sweet. But you go. I be all right."

A remark about idiots was on the tip of Fargo's tongue but instead he said, "Suit yourself. It's your blood that will be spilled." He turned and hurried around the tent. Vassily Baranof was bound to have heard the shots and just as bound to hurry back out of worry for his sister. Come to think of it, the Tlingits were bound to have heard them, as well, and the entire war party might be on its way to investigate.

Fargo was sorry he ever sat in on that poker game in Seattle. He was even sorrier he had won the pot. The thought made him grin. Winning pots was what poker was all about.

Suddenly a shadow separated itself from a nearby tent.

In reflex Fargo brought up the Henry. He would be damned if he would let the Russians or the Tlingits get their hands on him again. Now that he had his weapons, he was leaving, and anyone who tried to stop him would be welcome to digest lead.

"Don't shoot!" the shadow blurted. "It's me!"

Fargo held his fire. "Me" turned out to be Earl. Impossibly enough, he was dirtier than ever. His clothes and face were smeared with dirt, as if he had dug a hole and climbed in. "Where have you been?"

Earl gestured at the mountain behind him. "Up there, hid among the rocks. When that bastard killed Lester I knew it wouldn't be long before he got around to me, so I snuck off."

"You've been up there this whole time?"

"Where else would I be? I've been waiting for the chance to come down. I saw you, but then that bear showed up."

Fargo lowered the Henry. "I'm leaving. You are welcome to come with me if you want."

"But the gold!"

"You can have it," Fargo said. "If the Russians or the Tlingits or a bear or something else doesn't get you first."

"The Tlingits? What do they have to with this?"

Fargo refused to squander more time. "Come with me and I will explain." He took it for granted Earl would follow but when he glanced back Earl had not moved. "What are you waiting for? The Russians will be back any time now."

"I'm not leaving without some of the gold," Earl said. "I'm not going back to Sitka empty-handed."

"You won't be going back at all if you don't get the hell out of here," Fargo said.

"Go ahead. I'm not leaving."

Earl had a wild gleam in his eyes, a gleam Fargo recognized, the gleam of pure, raw greed. "Didn't you learn anything from Lester's death?"

"How dare you?" Earl bristled. "He was my partner, not yours. Him and me had been together ten years."

"Keep on as you are and you will be together again real soon," Fargo predicted. He did not wait for a reply. Maybe Earl did not care about dying, but he did. He was not ready to cash in his chips. Given his druthers, he would not mind living a good long while yet. There were a lot of places he had not seen, a lot of women he had not bedded.

Fargo came to the last tent. So far no shouts had broken the stillness of the night, which struck him as peculiar. Or maybe the Russians were farther off than he figured. He was about to plunge into the forest when a sound drew him up short. It came from the other end of the camp. An indistinct outcry, so faint he could not say whether it had been a woman or a man.

Fargo took another step toward the pines, then stopped. An awful premonition had wormed into his head. He assured himself he must be mistaken but he could not shake the certainty.

With an oath, Fargo spun and retraced his steps, running instead of walking. If he was wrong he was making a fool of himself. If he was right—well, he did not want to think of what might be happening if he was right. Surely not, he told himself. Surely Earl had more sense.

Another cry spurred Fargo to run faster. There was no doubt now. He should have suspected, but then, Earl had always been after the gold and nothing but the gold.

A lantern had been lit in Vassily Baranof's tent. It backlit their silhouettes. She was still alive, kicking and struggling, and she saw Fargo when he exploded into the tent and raised the Henry.

Earl had his back to the flap. But Kira's expression warned him. Releasing her throat, he spun. Lust contorted his features. He was unarmed, which was the only thing that saved him.

"The gold, huh?" Fargo said.

Kira rolled out of Earl's reach. Gasping and rubbing her throat, she rose to her knees. "Shoot him!" she mewed. "He try take my sex!"

Beads of sweat peppered Earl's brow. Licking his thick lips, he stared into the Henry's muzzle and said, "I wasn't really going to hurt her. I only want, you know." He grinned as if it were a big joke a fellow male would appreciate.

"If I had not come back, you would have killed her." Fargo made it a statement of fact, not a question.

"No, no, no. I just said. A few pokes wouldn't hurt the bitch. Besides, she's Russian, so where is the harm?"

Fargo's trigger finger itched. Moving to one side, he said grimly, "I would shut up and run if I were you. I would run very fast and get as far from here as you can before I change my mind."

Kira waved a hand at Earl. "No! Shoot him! He like animal! Worse animal than bear!"

His lust replaced by fear, Earl sidled toward the flap. "I'll go, I'll go," he said. "Just don't pull that trigger."

"Kill him!" Kira urged. She was red in the face and had finger marks on her throat. "Kill bastard!"

"Go," Fargo said. "Go now."

Bobbing his multiple chins, Earl turned and pushed on the flap and bounded from the tent. But he had taken only a step and still had hold of the flap when there was a fleshy *thwack-thwack-thwack* and he stopped as if he had slammed into a brick wall.

"What?" Kira wondered.

Earl backed into the tent. His arms had fallen limp and he was gaping at three feathered shafts that jutted from his chest. The arrows were newly made and unmarked so no one could trace them to their makers. He reached for one but could not lift his arm high enough. He looked at Fargo and tried to speak but all that came out of his mouth was blood. From his mouth and from his nose, copious dark rivulets flowed down over his chins.

"Indians!" Kira shrieked.

"I warned you," Fargo said. He dashed to the lantern and blew it out. When he turned, Earl lay on the ground, feebly twitching.

"What we do?" Kira asked. "I not want to die."

"*Now* you think of that?" Fargo shook his head and moved nearer to the flap. He did not open it. Not when he was bound to be greeted with a swarm of shafts.

From outside came a familiar voice. "Do you hear me, clever one? I know you are in there."

"I hear you, Gray Fox," Fargo answered. It was pointless not to.

"Is the fat one dead?"

"Very," Fargo said.

"We have surrounded the tent. There is no escape. Throw the rifle and the revolver out and step out with your hands where we can see them. You and the female, together."

"If I don't?" Fargo asked. He was stalling. The answer was as plain as the dead man bristling with arrows.

"We will kill you whether you do or whether you do not. But we will kill you much more slowly if you do not. Slowly, and with great pain."

"So my not being Russian no longer matters?"

"It never did," Gray Fox said. "I like you, but we cannot leave witnesses to our vengeance."

"The woman dies, too, then?"

"I am sorry."

"So am I," Fargo said, "because the only way you are getting your hands on my hardware is if you pry them from my fingers."

"There are more than thirty of us and only one of you," Gray Fox pointed out. "How long do you think you can last?"

Fargo thumbed back the Henry's hammer. "Let's find out."

17

A commotion broke out. The Tlingits yelled to one another in their own tongue. Then Gray Fox said something and it grew quiet.

Fargo backed away from the flap. Taking Kira's hand, he moved to the middle of the tent and crouched. She followed his example, the whites of her eyes showing.

"What do they do?"

"Your guess is as good as mine," Fargo said so only she would hear. Whatever it was, more blood was bound to be spilled.

Yet another irony. Fargo had no personal quarrel with the Tlingits. He did not want to harm any of them, any more than he wanted to be harmed by them. They were letting their hatred for the Russians taint their view toward all whites. The result: here he was, forced to defend his life over something someone else had done decades ago. The thought prompted him to shout, "Gray Fox!"

"I hear you, American."

"Your fight is not with me. It is with the Russians. Let me leave and take the lady with me and no one need be hurt."

"You will tell the government what we have done. Captain Petrov will come with soldiers to punish us."

"I will tell no one. You have my word."

There was silence before the old Tlingit said, "I believe you, American. I sense you speak with a true tongue. Very well. I will let you go. But the woman stays. She is Russian."

Fargo heard Kira gasp.

"You not leave me," she pleaded. "They kill me. Maybe do like other man tried."

"What is your answer, American?" Gray Fox called.

Fargo sighed. "As you say, she is a woman. I can't go off and leave her to be butchered."

"That is too bad," Gray Fox said.

"Warriors do not make war on women," Fargo tried a different tack. "Can't you find it in you to let her live?"

"No, American, I cannot. I have already explained. The Russians have done terrible things to our women. I will not spare one of theirs."

"But she didn't do anything to you or yours," Fargo noted. "Why punish an innocent?"

"Our women, our children, were just as innocent, but that did not stop the Russians. They must now taste their own cruelty."

"Don't do this, Gray Fox. I'm asking you man to man."

"I am sorry, American. Some things must be whether we want them to be or not. Another time, I would be glad to call you a friend. But here and now, you defend my enemy, and in doing so, you become an enemy."

Silence fell again, all the more unnerving because Fargo did not know what form the attack would take. He found out when a bow twanged and an arrow sliced through the canvas on the right side of the tent, buzzed within a foot of his face, and embedded itself in the ground near the left side.

Kira blurted words in Russian and made as if to rise and run out of the tent but Fargo yanked her back down beside him.

"That was the first of many, American," Gray Fox said. "It will not be pleasant. Give up and I promise your death will be quick and with little pain."

"Go to hell," Fargo replied.

Another bow string twanged. This time the arrow came through the left wall of the tent and missed Fargo and the woman by no more than four inches. It stuck in the ground, quivering.

"One last time, American. I have no wish for you to suffer."

"Do you know what a hypocrite is?" Fargo rejoined.

Gray Fox let out a sigh. "Very well. I have tried. It is on your head, not mine. Good-bye, American."

Motioning to Kira, Fargo flattened and crawled to the rear. She was so scared she practically glued herself to him, and twice he had to push her off his arm so he could crawl unhindered.

Behind them, arrows pierced the tent, first from the right side and then from the left. Five, six, seven arrows, several striking the center in the spots where Fargo and Kira had just been.

"Are you ready to give up now?" Gray Fox shouted.

Fargo did not answer. He had reached the back of the tent. Rising partway, he drew the toothpick.

"American?"

Inserting the razor tip into the canvas, Fargo cut downward. He cut slowly, quietly, so the Tlingits who were bound to be watching the rear of the tent would not hear.

"American, are you alive?" Gray Fox asked.

Fargo made a six-inch slit. Removing the knife, he carefully pried the slit open using two fingers, and peeked out. Two dusky warriors were ten feet away. It was dark here at the back of the tent, and the pair had not seen the knife or heard the faint rasp of steel on canvas.

"American?"

Fargo resumed cutting. Faster now, since he could watch the pair as he cut, and when one or the other looked at the tent, he would freeze until they looked away.

"Woman, are you alive in there?"

Any moment now, Gray Fox would send a warrior in,

or come in himself. Fargo had cut almost to the bottom. Now he cut at right angles, parallel to the ground. He was ready. But he did not make his break. Not just yet.

Gray Fox was saying something in the Tlingit tongue.

The front flap rustled, and a warrior stuck his head in.

Twisting, Fargo fired. He did not aim high or low. They were out to kill him. They would get what they deserved. He aimed at where the man's chest should be, and scored, for at the boom of his rifle the warrior jerked and a sharp cry filled the tent. Instantly, Fargo turned to the rear canvas and shoved his head and shoulders through.

The two Tlingits were not looking down. They had moved to the left and were staring along the side of the tent, trying to see what was going on up front.

Fargo shot them. He sent a slug into the head of one and as the second turned he put a slug into the man's ear. Then he was out and on his feet and reaching down to help Kira.

Harsh shouts rose, and feet drummed the ground. A warrior appeared at the corner, a spear at his shoulder.

Fargo fired, coring the wide chest. He pushed Kira toward the forest and backpedaled, covering them as a jumble of yells testified to the confusion rampant among the Tlingits.

An arrow whizzed past Fargo's ear. He fired at the right corner of the tent to discourage the bowman from trying again. Then pines were around them, and turning, he grasped Kira and ran. For once she did not argue. There was nothing like having someone try to kill you to make a person come to their senses.

Gray Fox was shouting. Any moment now, and the Tlingits would give chase, a pack of painted wolves who would not be satisfied with anything less than the blood of their quarry.

Alone, Fargo stood a better chance of eluding them. His woodlore was second to none. Kira, on the other hand, made more noise than a panicked doe. But he would not desert her. Not to the fate the Tlingits had in store. It was not in him.

So they ran. Fargo held on to her hand. He caught her when she stumbled, which she did frequently. She was terrified, and breathed in great gasps, even when he whispered to her to try to be more quiet. Every so often she would say, to herself and not to him, "I not want to die." She did not notice that she said it in English and not Russian.

The Tlingits were after them. Each was as quiet as Fargo in moving through the woods, but there were thirty of them, or thereabouts, and they could not help the random rustle of a leaf or a blade of grass or the crunch of a dry leaf or the snap of a twig. The sounds warned Fargo the warriors were spreading out to form a human net from which there would be no escape and no retreat.

Let them come, was Fargo's reaction. He had done all he could to avoid bloodshed. He had assured them he was not their enemy but they paid no heed. The lives of those he had shot, and the lives of those he would take if they tried to take his, were on their shoulders, not his.

Kira stumbled yet again, and Fargo caught her and swept her upright. She tried to rub her shin but he pulled her after him, whispering, "We can't slow down."

"But I hurt," she whined.

"You will hurt a lot worse with an arrow stuck in you."

That goaded her to greater speed, and for close to ten minutes they made swift progress. Fargo was adept at avoiding obstacles others might not have missed. A downed branch here, a log there, then a small boulder. He had the starlight to thank. Enough filtered through. Otherwise, they would blunder about in pitch black and collide with everything in their path.

The brush behind them crackled. Fargo whirled as out of it shot a stocky shape with an upraised double-bladed knife. Fargo fired the Henry one-handed from the hip, and the stocky shape catapulted backward into the brush and did not stir.

Shouts came from the right and left. The Tlingits had him pinpointed and were converging.

Fargo nearly wrenched Kira's arm from her socket. He

rounded a spruce and crossed a small clearing and then was in among trees again. An arrow struck a trunk with a loud *thunk*.

Fargo veered to the left, went a dozen feet, and angled to the right. He had lost track of how far they had run but he would imagine it was a quarter of a mile if not more. If he had to, he could run for miles yet. But Kira could not. Her legs were giving out. She was stumbling more than ever, and she was breathing more heavily, not from fright but from fatigue. She confirmed it with her next gasp.

"My legs much tired."

"Keep going if you can," Fargo urged.

"I sorry," Kira said, and slowed.

Fargo pulled but she did not have it in her. Just then a knee-high log appeared. He slid over it, helped her do the same, and sank to the dank earth, his arm around her shoulder. "Not a peep," he whispered in her ear. "We are dead if you make a sound."

A bob of her head showed she understood the gravity.

Out of the night they came, bounding like two-legged wolves. Some passed close to the log, others farther away. None came right up to it. And when the last of them had gone by, when minutes had passed and no more appeared, Fargo slowly rose and sat on the log.

Kira sat beside him. She was breathing easier but she was exhausted and still scared.

"Are us safe?"

"For the time being."

"I be so afraid," Kira whispered. "Hear many stories for savages. They do terrible things. Every should die." In her extremity, her English was worse than ever.

Fargo looked at her. "Their women and children, too?"

"All," Kira insisted, then frowned. "No. That not be right. Not women. Never little children." Her brow knit and she pondered and finally said, "Why can't all white and red be nice?"

"Hell if I know." Fargo thought of his usual haunts, where hate was just as common. But he couldn't wait to get back there. "I aim to take the first ship to Seattle," he said to himself. From there he would strike off for the central Rockies. A couple of weeks in the high country sounded like heaven.

"You miss America?" Kira asked.

"I miss being alone," Fargo said.

"You no like people?"

"They wear on the nerves." Fargo did not elaborate. Let her think what she wanted. "Have you caught your breath?"

"Caught it?" Kira said, then grinned. "Oh. You Americans be funny how you say things. Yes, I have my breath caught."

"No talking. We will go slow. Keep your eyes peeled." Fargo rose, clasping her hand in his. He started off but she did not move.

"American?"

"I have a name," Fargo said. Not that anyone in Alaska ever used it. "What now?"

"You mad with me?" Kira whispered.

"No madder than I am at myself." Again Fargo led her off and this time she fell into step. The forest was still but the stillness was deceptive. The Tlingits could be anywhere.

Kira was more sure-footed now that they were taking their time. She did not bump into things, and tripped only once. They had gone slightly over a mile by Fargo's reckoning and were near the gurgling stream when she brushed against him and whispered in his ear.

"Sabina say you be great lover."

Fargo stared at her.

Kira smiled coyly. "Maybe you and me do like her and you do."

"Women," Fargo said.

"Sorry?"

Whatever answer Fargo might have given was cut short by figures that rose up out of the high grass. A brawny hand gripped the Henry's barrel before Fargo could raise it while at the same instant a pair of iron arms wrapped around his own, pinning them to his side. He kicked at the man holding the Henry but the man nimbly dodged. Then there were six or seven hemming him, and resisting was pointless.

Another figure appeared. He strode up to Fargo and relieved Fargo of the Colt. "Surprised to see me again, American?" Vassily Baranof asked with a sneer. "I promised you an early grave and I am a man of my word."

18

"Vassily!" Kira cried, and threw her arms around his neck. "Oh, Vassily, I am sorry much for you." Pressing her face to his chest, she began crying.

Vassily said something to her in Russian and when she did not respond he glanced sharply at Fargo. "What is she talking about? What does she have to be sorry about?"

"She is sorry about your sister," Fargo said.

Stiffening, Vassily pried Kira from him. "Sabina? Something has happened to Sabina?"

Sobbing and sniffling, Kira nodded.

"What? Tell me, woman, before I lose my temper."

Kira wailed and pressed her tear-streaked face to his chest again.

Fargo girded himself. The Russians who were holding him were distracted by the exchange between their leader and Kira, and their grips had slackened. The man with the Henry was holding it loosely.

Vassily turned to Fargo again. "So help me, if one of you does not start talking—" He did not finish his threat.

"Your sister is dead," Fargo revealed. He was unprepared for what transpired next.

"You killed her?" Vassily snarled. He reached out for Fargo's throat but he was still holding the Colt. Tossing it to the man holding the Henry, he raged, "I will twist your neck with my bare hands!"

Jerking his head back, Fargo said, "It was a brown bear, not me. I had no reason to kill her."

Vassily straightened in shock. Whirling, he shook Kira again, twice as hard. "Is this true? Speak, damn you, woman! I have had enough of your weeping."

"It very true!" Kira got out between sobs. "Bear kill her. It kill also man who guard us. Indians kill other one."

"Indians?" Vassily drew back, perplexed. "What Indians? We have not seen any. You do not make sense."

Kira nodded at Fargo. "Ask him. He saw."

"The Tlingits killed Earl," Fargo confirmed. "They trailed you all the way from Sitka."

Vassily was still confused. "Why would they do that?"

"They want you dead," Fargo said. "You and everyone with you. Something to do with something your grandfather did to them and the Aleuts."

"How can this be?" Appearing dazed, Vassily took a step back. "My sister, dead? The Tlingits making war?"

"We shouldn't stand here like this," Fargo warned. "They can pick us off." When he said "us" he meant him. "Get into the trees before it is too late."

It was already too late.

There was the *swish* of displaced air, and the Russian holding the Henry and the Colt was jolted by a hardwood spear that struck him below the sternum and transfixed his torso from front to back. The man had life enough left to glance down and bleat in Russian. Then he keeled over.

The rest of Baranof's men were rooted in disbelief. But only until arrows and more spears started raining down. Some of the shafts did not find targets. Others did. Within seconds men were shouting and screaming and firing wildly in all directions.

One of the men holding Fargo took an arrow in the arm and let go. The other released him and leaped back to spray lead.

Artificial thunder pealed the length and breadth of the valley.

Vassily was bellowing in Russian, evidently for them to hold their fire, but most were too spooked to heed or did not hear him.

Kira had her hands to her ears and was screeching in terror.

In all the bedlam and confusion it was simple for Fargo to hunker and reclaim the Henry and the Colt. No one tried to stop him. None of the Russians were even looking at him. Kira turned and clung to Vassily.

Fargo holstered the Colt, swiveled, and spied the tree line. If the Russians wanted to stay in the open and be picked off one by one that was their business. He had other notions.

Staying low, Fargo zigzagged toward the pines. A lead hornet buzzed his head. He looked back thinking one of the Russians was trying to stop him. But no, they were still blistering the night with wild shots. He ran on and ducked behind the first trunk he came to.

Many of the Russians had emptied their rifles and were reloading. The hail of arrows and spears had stopped, and from the smiles and looks the Russians were giving one another, they thought they had driven the Tlingits off. They were mistaken.

A howl uncannily like that of a wolf ululated on the wind. It was a signal. Out of the woods poured the Tlingits, their bows and lances set aside in favor of their double-bladed knives, clubs, and axes. Not hatchets, like the plains tribes commonly used, but long-handled axes that could sever a head or a limb with a single swing. And sever a head one did. Fargo saw it come sailing toward him. It bounced twice before rolling to a stop.

Fargo wedged the Henry to his shoulder. He did not want to take sides. But of the two, the Russians, in his estimation, were the lesser evil. So when he saw a Tlingit about to stab Pyotr in the back, he shot the warrior in the head.

Pyotr had been knocked down. Now he rose and glanced

about, and since he had some idea which direction the shot came from, he spotted Fargo. If he was surprised he did not show it but instantly leaped up and ran toward him.

Pyotr was not the only one. Holding tight on to Kira's hand, Vassily Baranof raced for the trees. He had a revolver but he did not use it.

A Tlingit rushed out of the night behind them. Vassily did not seem to notice him. Neither did Kira. Fargo did, and a hasty shot sent the warrior pitching to the soil.

Vassily and the girl made it. They crouched near Fargo, and Vassily said, "That was you who saved us?"

"I wasn't thinking straight," Fargo said.

The combat had become general. Man pitted against man, Russian invader against hate-filled warrior. Knives and axes flashed. Guns boomed. Men screamed and cursed.

Fargo got out of there. He had done what he could, and the way down the valley was open. He ran, counting on the Russians to keep the Tlingits busy. But he had not counted on some of the Russians fleeing with him, Vassily, Kira, and Pyotr among them.

It was hellacious, that flight. The dark and the press of vegetation and the uncertainty of never knowing when a Tlingit might rear up. They ran until they were spent and then they ran some more.

His lungs fit to burst, Fargo stopped and doubled over with his hands on his knees. The few warriors who had come after them had inexplicably fallen back. He did not like that. The Tlingits would not give up so easily.

Vassily and Pyotr and the other Russians were also bent over, some with spittle dribbling over their chins, all on the point of collapse. Kira was on her side on the ground, groaning.

Fargo could not resist. "So much for the gold," he said.

Gulping air, Vassily shook his head. "I will come back," he replied. "I will bring twice as many men."

"Some folks never learn," Fargo taunted. No amount of gold was worth dying for.

"You would let primitives with bows and knives scare

you off?" Vassily retorted. "You Americans, you are not bold enough. Your country will never amount to much."

"We should be more like you, is that it?"

Vassily was breathing a little easier, and straightened. "Now that you mention it. I am not timid, like you. When I see something I want, I take it, and I crush everything that stands in my way."

Fargo counted eleven Russians. "Seems to me the Tlingits are doing the crushing. Another attack and you won't have any men left."

"They caught us by surprise," Vassily said. "They will not catch us by surprise again." He sniffed in indignation. "I rarely make mistakes."

"Tell that to your sister."

Vassily Baranof became a statue. When next he spoke, his tone was laced with resentment. "For that slight, when this is over, you will die in excruciating pain."

Fargo unfurled and trained the Henry on him. "I should drop you right here and be done with it." But the shot might be heard by the Tlingits, who were bound to be searching for them.

Vassily laughed. "Go ahead. I do not fear death, American. I do not fear anyone or anything."

Fargo had had enough. Enough of the Russians, enough of the Tlingits, enough of the valley, and enough of Alaska. Covering them, he began to back away. "I'm leaving. I suggest you don't follow me."

"Do not worry. I refuse to tuck my tail between my legs and slink off like a cur," Vassily said. "I will wait for daylight and then show the primitives why my grandfather was so widely feared by their fathers and their father's fathers."

Fargo frowned in disgust. Whites who thought they had the God-given right to lord it over the red man had caused more sorrow and loss of life than could be calculated. About to back into the trees, he stopped when Kira said his name.

"I want going with you."

"What about your friends?"

"Yes, what about us," Vassily said. "You belong by

our side. I would take it poorly, most poorly indeed, if you run off with this American." He added something in Russian.

Kira wrung her hands. "Please, Vassily, do not be so. You and me be close."

"Is that what you think?" Vassily snorted. "You were Sabina's friend, never mine. To me all you were and all you will ever be is a way to keep warm on a cold night."

"Oh, Vassily," Kira said.

"Oh, Kira," Vassily mimicked her. "Surely you did not think I cared for you? Any more than I would care for any other tart? That is where my sister met you, was it not? In a saloon?"

Kira's eyes were glistening with tears. "All this time," she said softly. "How could I so mistake you?"

"As always, your English is atrocious, my dear," Vassily said, and launched into more Russian. She responded a few times, mostly in monosyllables. Finally Vassily spat on the ground and barked in English, "Fine, then. Go with the American. I wash my hands of you. I hope the savages get their hands on you. Maybe after they have tortured you and you are close to dying, you will realize the mistake you made."

Hanging her head, Kira came to Fargo. "Thank you. I try keeping up."

Fargo took her hand. He kept one eye on the Russians but Vassily did not try to stop them. When they were out of sight and out of earshot, he asked, "What did he say to you back there?"

"He call me whore," Kira said sorrowfully. "He call me ugly things. Him say he never like me. Only tolerate me." She paused. " 'Tolerate,' that be the right word?"

Fargo nodded.

"He only tolerate because Sabina like me," Kira went on. "Now she am gone, he not want me near."

"But he wanted you to stay with him."

"Only so not be with you." Kira raised her eyes to the stars. Tears were trickling down her cheeks. "I want be in Sitka again. I want drink. I want sleep in soft bed."

Fargo could use a drink himself. But on foot it would take weeks to get there. Weeks of hard travel over some of the most rugged terrain anywhere. That the country-side was crawling with man-eating beasts and hostiles only made a bad situation worse.

Now that Fargo thought about it, he would not mind Kira's company half as much as he thought he would. Those cold nights Vassily mentioned were all too real in the wild, and they did not have any blankets. They did not have any supplies at all. But that did not worry Fargo nearly as much as the Tlingits. He was accustomed to living off the land. He had been doing it for so long that it was second nature. They would not go hungry. They would not lack for water. But it would still be rough going on foot.

"Wish I had gun," Kira said out of the blue.

Fargo would not mind if she did. Two rifles were better than one, even if she could not hit the broad side of a charging moose.

"You not say much," Kira remarked.

"I am listening," Fargo said. And he was. The Tlingits were bound to be after them, and the brown bear he had slain might not be the only one that roamed the valley. But so far he had not heard anything out of the ordinary.

"I sorry," Kira said. "Me not think."

Fargo thought of all she had been through, and sought to soothe her by saying, "It's all right. You are doing fine."

They picked up the pace, but not so fast as to wear them out before morning. The hours crawled by. By the position of the North Star it was about one when Fargo led her to the stream and announced, "We will rest a spell."

"Thank you." Kira gratefully sank down and immediately began cupping water to her mouth.

"Not too much," Fargo cautioned. "It might make you sick."

"I be careful," Kira responded. "I not be water pig."

Fargo was beginning to take a shine to her. She had

an earnest simplicity he liked. He thought of the shapely contours of her body, and promptly banished the image from his brain. Now was not the time for that.

From up the valley came the cry of a night bird that was not a night bird. It was answered by another night bird that was not a bird, only much closer to them.

Kira's head shot up. Water dripping from her chin, she asked, "Are they—?"

"Indians," Fargo confirmed.

"They be after us?"

"After us and Vassily, both," Fargo said. He refrained from adding that Gray Fox would not rest until they were all dead. It was the only way for Gray Fox to ensure there were no reprisals against his people.

"Fargo, you like me?"

Fargo looked at her. "You ask the damnedest questions."

"Please. Do you? I like you much. But I think maybe you not like me much." Kira fluffed at her hair. "Is it I be not much pretty?"

Sinking to one knee, Fargo pulled her to him and kissed her full on the mouth. Kira uttered a tiny sigh and melted against him. Her lips were exquisitely soft. She was a far better kisser than Sabina. At length he drew back and asked, "Does that answer your question?"

"Thank you. I very need that."

Fargo chuckled. "You women. Here we are running for our lives and all you can think of is fooling around." Suddenly her grip on him tightened and her eyes grew wide. He spun, raising the Henry.

Something was coming through the grass toward them.

19

The thing was almost on them when Fargo saw it clearly. Lowering the Henry, he grimly smiled.

A small doe, coming to the stream to drink, veered aside and bounded off into the dark.

Kira uttered a nervous laugh. "I think maybe Indians." She placed a hand on his leg. "I also think of what be in your pants."

Fargo did something he had rarely done before "No. Not here. Not now. We are asking for trouble."

"But it be dark hours yet," Kira said. "And we alone."

"It's dark, all right," Fargo said. "Dark enough that the Tlingits or your friends could sneak up on us without us seeing." He grasped her hand and said more firmly, "No, and that's that."

Her shoulders slumping, Kira stood. "As say you, but I still want."

"We will rest until daylight and then push on," Fargo proposed as he led her into the forest. They had gone a short way when they had to climb over a downed tree. Fargo went first and helped her. He went to move on, then whispered, "Wait." When trees were uprooted, whether by a storm or age, they sometimes ripped out a lot of earth when they fell. He moved along the downed spruce until he came to the roots. Where the tree had once stood was a bowl-shaped depression about three feet deep and six feet wide. "This will do nicely."

"We rest in dirt?"

"No one can see us," Fargo pointed out, "and we will be out of the wind."

"Wind is important?"

"You don't want every meat eater for a mile around to pick up our scent, do you?" Fargo hopped down, held up his arms, and carefully lowered her beside him.

"Cozily spot," Kira said.

"I've slept in worse places," Fargo said, thinking of the time he was stranded high on a mountain during a blizzard and had to sleep in a snowbank, and another time when he was on foot in the desert and had to sleep in the open under the burning sun.

"Me well as." Kira sat with her back to the side of the bowl and her arms across her legs. "My dress be mess."

"You look just fine," Fargo said. Without thinking, he sat next to her. He propped the Henry beside him and leaned back. Until that moment he had not realized how worn out he was. He closed his eyes and stifled a yawn. "I will wake you at sunrise." No matter how tired he might be, he always woke up at the crack of dawn.

"As you wish." Kira leaned against him, her cheek on his arm, her hand on his hip.

Fargo had a knack for being able to sleep anywhere, anytime, under just about any circumstances. He started to doze off. The night sounds faded and a black veil shrouded his senses. Then suddenly he was awake again, and unsure what had awakened him until he felt pressure where there should not be any. Soft pressure, a gentle stroking, that had done what it always did, whether he was awake or asleep. "What do you think you're doing?"

Kira did not stop. "What it feel like?"

"I told you no."

"Your manly thing say yes."

"Damn it," Fargo said. But he did not push her hand away. Damn *him*, but it felt good. So good, he did not want her to stop. He closed his eyes and drifted on the surface of a sea of pleasure until he felt her fingers pry at his buckle. Gripping her hand, he looked at her and said, "My pants stay on." That was all he needed—to be literally caught by Vassily or the Tlingits with his pants down.

Kira smiled. "Can stay on and still fun make, yes?"

"Yes, but—" Fargo got no further. She had taken his hand and placed it on her left breast. Almost of their own accord his fingers closed and squeezed.

A low moan escaped Kira. Shifting, she pressed her body to his, her breath warm on his neck. "You I like much."

"We are loco, the both of us," Fargo said. But he did not stop fondling her globes.

"What be loco?" Kira asked.

"It means plumb crazy," Fargo enlightened her. "And only a crazy person would do what we are doing."

"People do all time," Kira teased, and nipped his chin with her teeth. "In Russia. In country you from. In queen country, England. In far Australia. In Norway."

"Norway?"

"I there once. Pretty men. Handsome women."

"You really need to work on your English."

Kira licked his ear. "Me work your something." She had his pants undone. "My, my. You like musk ox."

"That's a new one." Fargo shut her up by fusing his mouth to hers in a kiss that went on and on. He had to admit, he was suddenly not nearly as tired as he had been a short while ago.

"Mmmmmm," Kira cooed when they broke. "You great kiss man. I be much fond your tongue."

"I'm rather fond of it myself," Fargo admitted while tugging at her dress. She rose up to make it easier and the hem rose as high as her knees. He ran his fingers from her ankle to her thigh and felt her skin quiver. "Like that, do you?"

"I always like the touching," Kira whispered. "It best of anything."

She had something there, Fargo reflected as his hand slid higher. Her inner thigh was silken smooth and wonderfully warm. He slid his palm higher still, and was astounded to discover she did not wear undergarments. "All you have on is a dress?"

"I never care much for lot of clothes," Kira said. "If it be me, I wear only skin."

"That would be something to see." Fargo grinned and cupped her nether mount. At the contact, she gasped.

"Yes! Yes! There."

"Not so loud," Fargo said gruffly. It was bad enough they were doing it. If he had any sense he would stop and make her go to sleep. Instead, he ran the tip of his finger along her slit and found it moist and yielding.

"Ohhhhhhhhh," Kira breathed. "Do many times. Please."

"Hussy," Fargo said.

"What be that?"

"A woman who likes it many times," Fargo explained while lightly moving his finger.

"Then me much big hussy," Kira said. "Me biggest hussy ever."

"Shush," Fargo said, and thrust his finger up into her. She bit his shoulder; then her hot mouth rose to his. Their tongues entwined. Her inner walls were wet and grew wetter still as he pumped his finger in and out.

Fargo tried to focus on the night around them. He tried to stay alert for stealthy sounds, tried to listen for the cries of night birds that were not night birds. But the dirt hole and the woods and the night itself became a vague mist at the borders of his awareness. All he could feel was Kira's soft, luscious body, all he could hear were her coos and intakes of breaths. The sensation that he could never get enough of rose up within him. She had unleashed the need that he had earlier denied, and he had no desire to deny it now even if he could.

For once, though, Fargo did not want to prolong the sensation. His dulled senses made them vulnerable. They must get it over with quickly. To that end, he shifted, parted her thighs, and eased her onto his lap. She came willingly, even eagerly, and when he raised her up and aligned his iron pole, she grinned.

"Good stuff now."

Fargo put a finger to her lips. Kira placed her hands on his shoulders, and nodded. Tensing, Fargo drove up into her as if seeking to impale her. Her reaction was to throw back her head and part her red lips. Fortunately, she had the presence of mind not to cry out or moan.

Their lips locked. Their hips rocked. Two bodies, moving as one, the tempo increasing as their passion climbed. They were breathing heavily but it could not be helped, any more than the inevitable result of their coupling could be helped.

Kira gushed first. She had wanted it badly, she had needed it badly, and her release tossed her on waves of rapture.

Cause and effect. Fargo's explosion rivaled hers. Raw pleasure engulfed him, the sublime pounding and the sweet sensual savor that obliterated all else. Afterward, he coasted to a stop, his skin cool with sweat.

Kira sagged against him, her head on his shoulder. "Thank you," she said softly. "I much needed that."

Stroking her hair, Fargo tilted his head back to listen. He heard only the wind and far to the north a lonesome wolf. Soon her breathing told him she was asleep, and he shut his eyes and settled back. He started to drift off. Another few moments and he would join her in slumber.

Somewhere nearby a twig snapped.

Instantly, Fargo was awake, the Henry in his hands. With Kira in his lap, he had to loop his arms around her to hold it, which proved awkward, but he did not shake her to wake her up. She might give a start and say something, and whoever or whatever broke the twig might hear her.

Fargo heard whispers, then the rustle of undergrowth. So it was a who and not a what and there was more than one of them. The language they were speaking left no doubt as to which who they were: Tlingits. By craning his neck, Fargo could see over the edge of the bowl. Warriors were on both sides. Seven or eight, all told. For a moment he thought they knew Kira and he were there but they crept past and moved off toward the stream.

Fargo sank back against the dank earth. That it was

not the entire war party told him the Tlingits had split into groups. The other groups could be anywhere. He closed his eyes and tried to fall asleep but seeing the Tlingits had his nerves on edge. He fidgeted. He shifted from side to side. His left leg developed a cramp, and try as he might, he could not get it to go away. He had no recourse but to gently ease Kira off his lap and lay her on her side. She mumbled and stirred but did not wake up. By vigorously rubbing his leg he soon relieved the cramp but his calf hurt for a while afterward.

Easing back, Fargo pulled his hat over his eyes. If he couldn't fall asleep he could at least sit there and rest quietly until the new day dawned. He listened to a coyote, he listened to the wind. The next thing he knew, a bird chirped, and he sat up in alarm, thinking it was not a bird but a Tlingit. The sparrow perched in a nearby hemlock set his worry to rest.

Dawn was breaking. The sky to the east had brightened and a pink band framed the horizon. The sparrow he had heard was not the only bird greeting the new day with song.

Fargo stretched and froze. He had heard a footstep. Grabbing the Henry, he pushed onto his knees and rose for a look-see. He could not help grinning. He had heard a step, all right. Several elk had been to the stream to slake their thirst and were now moving back into the heavy timber.

"What is it?" Kira fearfully asked. Her hair was a mess and her dress was worse but she looked terribly inviting lying there with her dress up around her thighs and her bosom straining against her bodice.

"Morning, sleepyhead," Fargo said. "Some elk are paying their regards."

"Sleepy-what?" Kira said. She rose to see, and smiled. "For so big make quiet steps."

When the elk were out of sight, Fargo stood. He had not wanted to spook them. He climbed out of the hole and lowered his arm for Kira to grab hold. For a full-bodied woman she was surprisingly light. He brushed dirt from his buckskins and she smoothed her dress, and together they cautiously moved toward the stream.

"What we do after drink and wash?" Kira whispered.

"We need horses," Fargo said. But the Tlingits had all of them, and they were not about to part with them willingly.

"How we find some?" Kira inquired.

"Leave that to me."

They came on a small pool. Fargo stood guard while she bathed. She did not care if he turned his back, so he didn't. Removing her dress, she gingerly stepped into the water, shivering from the cold. She could stand to be in for only a minute; then out she came, shaking and grinning. The sight of her naked body dripping with glistening drops was enough to start him stirring. He turned his back to her so she wouldn't notice.

With a female's instincts for such things, Kira teased him as she picked up her dress. "Why you not look, pretty man?"

"Once you've seen one naked woman, you've seen them all," Fargo said.

"I think you—what is word?—big fibber."

"I think you're right."

Fargo gave her the Henry and had her stand on the bank while he stripped off his buckskin shirt and washed his chest and face. The water was liquid ice. He broke out in goose bumps and heard Kira giggle. Quickly finishing, he shook his shirt out, donned it, placed his hat back on his head, reclaimed the Henry, and was ready. Almost. "You have a decision to make."

"Sorry?"

"You can come with me or you can hide in the hole until I get back," Fargo said. "You will be safer in the hole," he added.

"Where you go?" Kira asked.

"I told you. We need horses."

"Why you not want me go? You think maybe they catch you? You think maybe you not come back?"

All Fargo did was shrug.

Kira smiled and reached out and tenderly caressed his cheek. "You sweet, musk ox American."

Fargo laughed.

"What?"

"Nothing. What will it be?"

"The hole or go for you? You I pick." Kira hooked her arm in his and beamed like a girl going on a romantic stroll. "When you ready, I ready."

The sun was a golden crown on the rim of the world. Stubborn patches of darkness clung to the forest floor and would not be dispelled until the sun was fully risen.

Fargo headed up the valley. He figured the horses might be at the hollow the Tlingits had taken him to after they caught him. It would not take more than an hour to get there. He told Kira.

"That be good." Kira grinned happily and pecked his cheek.

Suddenly they both heard it. The whinny of one of the horses they were looking for.

Fargo glanced up and swore.

The horse was not alone. There were five of them, and on each was a painted warrior.

20

"Oh, hell," Fargo said. He did not want more trouble. The Tlingits' fight was with the Russians, not with him. Smiling, he raised his hand in friendly greeting.

One of the Tlingits pointed at Kira and said something that caused all of them to heft their weapons.

Fargo snapped the Henry to his shoulder. He had forgotten. He was *with* a Russian. In their eyes, that made him as much an enemy as Kira. "Run," he said to her. "Get to cover."

The Tlingits whooped and slapped their legs against their mounts. All five bore down at a gallop. Two had bows, and they were the first two Fargo shot. Two more had spears that looked more suitable for spearing fish than spearing people but that did not make them any less dangerous. Fargo squeezed the trigger and a slug smashed into the chest of the first. He swiveled to shoot the second and slipped on the dew-slick grass. He did not fall but it threw off his aim. Instantly, he jacked the Henry's lever to feed another cartridge into the chamber.

The warrior's arm whipped in an arc. He made an incredible throw. The spear cleaved the bright morning air in a high arc.

Fargo had plenty of time to sidestep, and did so as the spear was descending. He would never know why Kira did what she did next. Maybe she thought he was glued in shock. Whatever her reason, she cried, "No!" and pushed him. In doing so, she threw herself off balance. Before she could recover, the spear caught her under her arm and sheared through her body like a hot brand through wax. The iron tip burst out the other side, below her ribs.

"Oh!" Kira looked down in amazement. "I think I be dead," she said softly, and pitched to her knees.

A red haze fell before Fargo's eyes. He shot the warrior who had thrown the spear, worked the lever, shifted, and shot the last warrior.

Kira's chin was on her bosom, her arms limp. She did not stir when Fargo placed a hand on her arm and sank to a knee. Her eyes were open but unseeing. He felt her neck for a pulse but there was none.

Fargo bowed his head. He had not wanted any part of this. He had tried, truly tried, to avoid spilling blood, and what had it gotten him? All those he halfway liked were dead.

A whinny brought Fargo out of himself. Several of the horses had not run off. He walked to a sorrel and swung up. He did not mind the lack of a saddle. He had ridden bareback plenty of times. A jab of his heels, and he brought the sorrel to a gallop. He did not head down the valley and toward distant Sitka, but up it, toward the Tlingits and the Russians.

It was not ten minutes before Fargo came on three more warriors. At the sight of him, one yipped and all three rushed to be the first to the kill. He shot them dead, one after the other.

Fargo rode on. He did not know how many of the war party were left. He had accounted for quite a few, the Russians had undoubtedly slain a few more. He would guess at least twenty still roved the valley. That was an awful lot of warriors, but he had more than enough ammo.

Taking the box from his pocket, Fargo reloaded.

The sun was over an hour high when the sounds of battle wafted to Fargo's ears. Shots and screams and yells and the strident whinny of horses, a bedlam of death that drew him like a beacon. He slowed as he drew near.

Apparently, the Russians had been caught in a stand of aspens near the stream. Cut off from the forest, they had been surrounded. A half dozen bodies in tunics and paint lay in the grass around the aspens, along with two dead Russians.

Furtive movement in the aspens proved that some of the Russians were still alive. Tlingits were visible in the woods a few hundred feet from the stand. But they had learned their lesson and were not eager to cross the open space in the face of Russian rifles.

Fargo circled to come up behind the Tlingits. He rode at a walk and stopped often to scan the vegetation. He need not have worried. The Tlingits were so intent on the Russians, they did not spot him. He drew rein fifty feet from where Gray Fox exhorted the other warriors on. Evidently they were girding for another charge.

Fargo raised the Henry, then lowered it again. He waited. He was in no hurry. He would take his time and do it right.

In a short while, the Tlingits climbed on their horses and moved to the tree line. They stopped, and Gray Fox cupped a hand to his mouth and shouted in Russian.

Vassily Baranof answered.

Fargo could not tell what they were saying but their tone gave some clues. Gray Fox taunted the Russians, maybe saying they would all soon be dead. Vassily responded with defiance. Then, to Fargo's mild surprise, Gray Fox switched to English.

"I hear you, Russian dog. But know this. The blood of my son cries out for the blood of all your kind."

"You are a fool, old man," Vassily returned. "A liar, as well. You do not do this for your son. He died decades ago. No, you do this because of your granddaughter."

"You know, then," Gray Fox said.

"I had nothing to do with it," Vassily shouted.

"Now which one of us is the liar?"

"She came to me. She said she wanted to make money

the way my Russian girls do. She did not give me her real name but I knew who she was. I put her up in a shack down by the docks with the other Indian women who work for me." Vassily laughed. "That is what set you off, isn't it, old man? Your own granddaughter, spreading her legs for money."

Gray Fox did not reply.

"You blame me for her selling her body?" Vassily went on. "But it was her decision. I never approached her. Hell, I can't stand your kind. The only reason I have any Indian girls at all working for me is because some men like them. The men say they make love like animals."

"You are a pig," Gray Fox yelled. "You prey on the innocent and have no regrets."

"There are none of us innocent, old man. Your granddaughter least of all. Maybe if you live, you should visit her in her shack. Bring money and she might spread her legs for you."

"For that," Gray Fox said solemnly, "you will take a long time dying."

"Your threats do not scare me, old one," Vassily baited him. "We have guns and you do not, and if I have to, I will save a bullet for myself. You will not have the pleasure of torturing me."

"Just so you die," Gray Fox said. "Whether I do this for my son or my granddaughter or both, the important thing is that the taint of the Baranofs ends with you, Vassily Baranof."

"Come, then, you and those fools with you. You will find that no matter what you think of me, the Baranofs die like men."

Gray Fox addressed the Tlingits in their own language. Half a dozen bows were raised and arrows nocked to sinew strings.

Fargo stayed where he was. The two sides deserved what was coming to them. As far as he was concerned, they could butcher one another to the last man. They had brought it down on their own heads.

At a signal from Gray Fox, the bowmen let fly. They

immediately slid new arrows from their quivers and launched a second flight, doing it so fast, the second six were in the air before the first six arced down on the aspens.

Gray Fox bellowed in the Tlingit tongue and the war party swept toward the stand. Unlike the Sioux or the Comanches, who often whooped and hollered when they attacked, the Tlingits fought in deadly silence.

From the aspens came a scream. At least one of the arrows had scored. On its heels came a shout from Vassily Baranof and then a ragged volley that spewed lead and smoke. One of the Tlingits clutched his chest and toppled and another twisted to the impact of a heavy slug in his arm but the rest reached the stand unscathed.

Fargo still did not move.

The clash was fierce and noisy. Guns boomed, men shrieked and cursed. A riderless horse bolted out of the stand, its back smeared scarlet. A Russian staggered into view, an arrow in his belly. He fell to his knees, and probably never noticed the painted warrior who dashed up behind him and bashed out his brains with a war club.

Grinning in triumph, the warrior started to turn to go back into the stand.

Quick as thought, Fargo snapped the Henry to his shoulder and fired. The slug caught the Tlingit high in the chest and spun him completely around. He was dead before he struck the ground.

Another riderless horse crashed out of the stand and fled to the south.

The bedlam reached a crescendo. The outcome had been decided, and fewer guns were banging.

Suddenly Vassily Baranof burst into the open. His coat was torn and his shirt was bloody and his pants had a long tear in them. Backpedaling, he fired into the aspens, a fierce grin lighting his features.

After him came Pyotr and Fedor. The former had a gash on his left cheek and was limping. The latter had a feathered shaft jutting from his shoulder and was a portrait in terror.

Tlingits spilled out of the trees after them. Pyotr shot

two and then was overhauled by three more who stabbed and chopped with their double-bladed knives. He screamed as he went down and went on screaming as they hacked him to pieces.

Fedor tried to run but a spear transfixed his leg. Howling in agony, he fell on his side. In desperation he attempted to pull the spear out but he was not strong enough. By then two warriors stood over him, their wicked knives glinting in the sunlight. Fedor looked up at them and whined like a puppy that knew it was about to be kicked. Strangely, though, they did not touch him.

That left Vassily. He had a revolver in each hand and was firing with cool precision. He had dropped four Tlingits and now five more, including Gray Fox, were almost on him. Vassily took deliberate aim at Gray Fox but the next instant an arrow sliced through his right knee and he buckled. The lead meant for Gray Fox flew into the blue vault of the sky instead.

Vassily did not give in to the pain. Gritting his teeth, he aimed at another warrior, only to have his arm struck by a war club. Four of the five warriors pounced, their numbers and weight too much for him. His arms and legs were pinned.

It was then that Gray Fox stepped forward. He was smiling, a smile as icy as the arctic north. "And now we have you," he said in English.

Why English instead of Russian, Fargo could not say, unless Gray Fox spoke English better than Russian and was well aware Vassily was fluent in it, as well.

Vassily surged against his captors but there were too many. "Do it!" he demanded. "Do not play with me as a cat would a mouse. Get it over with!"

"That would be foolish," Gray Fox said. "I have waited too long for this moment. Killing you quickly would spoil it."

Fedor was still on the ground. He was wringing his sleeve, his eyes misted with tears. He spoke in Russian.

"No. You do not get to live," Gray Fox answered in English. "You did not lift a weapon against us. That is true. But you are still our enemy." He flicked a finger across his throat, and just like that, one of the warriors whipped his razor-edged knife across the little chemist's.

Fedor bleated. That was the only sound he made, and he made it only once. He thrashed madly about, his hands over his throat in a vain bid to staunch the spray of his life's blood. His movements grew weaker and weaker and finally ceased altogether.

Vassily spat at Gray Fox but missed. "You are scum, all of you. He never hurt any of your kind."

"He worked for you. That was enough."

Although furious, Vassily did not waste himself trying to break free. "So what do you have in your cruel heart for me, savage? Cut me to bits as you did poor Pyotr? Gouge out my eyes and chop off my fingers? What torture boils in that heathen brain of yours?"

Gray Fox smiled. "I have given it much thought, white man." He gestured, and the Tlingits formed a ring around Vassily. All drew their wicked knives.

Fargo had heard enough. He walked the sorrel to the grass and let the reins drop. Dismounting, he made no effort to sneak up on them. He wanted them to see him. He wanted them to see it coming.

A warrior heard the sorrel stamp and glanced over his shoulder. At his sharp exclamation, they all faced around.

"You!" Gray Fox cried. "What do you want?"

Fargo raised the Henry, lined up the front sight with the rear sight and both sights on Gray Fox, and shot him through the head. For a few seconds the rest were paralyzed with shock. Then one shouted and they all bounded toward him.

Fargo shot one and aimed at a second and shot him and aimed at a third and shot him. Rapidly, methodically, he blasted warrior after warrior. He would drop one and another would leap over the body and keep coming. The fastest died first, then those not so fast, and finally the two who brought up the rear but were as game as their friends. By then he had emptied the Henry and drawn his Colt, and he killed the last of them when the man was almost at arm's length with a knife raised for a fatal thrust.

Vassily Baranof had sat up and was leaning on his hands. He laughed merrily as Fargo walked up to him. "You astound me, American! You killed them all! Every last one! It is over."

"Not quite," Fargo said, and pressed the Colt to the Russian's broad forehead.

"No!" Vassily cried.

"Yes." Fargo squeezed the trigger.

Later that day, Skye Fargo trotted out of the valley. He did not look back. He was thinking of ship passage to Seattle, and the Cork and Keg, and a willowy woman named Marie. That, and one last thing. Smacking his lips, he said to the horse, "I'm going to stay drunk for a week."

LOOKING FORWARD!
The following is the opening section from the next novel in the exciting *Trailsman* series from Signet:

THE TRAILSMAN #311
IDAHO IMPACT

Idaho Territory, 1860—a town of secrets,
a town of violence is dangerous
to the man seeking the truth.

Skye Fargo, pitching his poker hand into the middle of the table, said, "I'm out."

"Hey, Fargo," laughed the slicker in the red vest and handlebar mustache, "you can't quit. I'm makin' too much money off you."

Fargo frowned. "I wouldn't push it, mister."

"Guess he don't know who you are, Mr. Fargo," said the old-timer sitting to the left of Fargo. To the slicker, he said, "I wouldn't be gloatin', mister. This one, he don't suffer fools."

Fargo stood up. "I'm the fool here. Havin' a bad night and should've quit about an hour ago."

"I didn't mean anything by that," the slicker said. "I was just havin' a little fun with ya was all."

"Already forgotten," Fargo said. "You boys finish up your game. I'm going to stand guard over those bottles behind the bar."

The crowd in the Gold Mine saloon had thinned out as ten p.m. approached. The sheriff of Twin Forks wanted to keep his town peaceful. He figured that drunks were at their worst as the hour drew later. He wanted the streets empty by the time he turned the jail over to his deputy for the night.

Fargo was riding through on his way to Boise where he was to meet an old friend who was having problems with rustlers. The friend had learned that the range detective who'd been hired to keep the man's cattle safe was actually part of the rustling gang. Fargo would lend a hand and a gun if necessary.

Two beers and a shot of whiskey later, Fargo yawned, looking forward to the hotel room he planned to take for the night. He'd played cards a couple towns back and won decent money. He still had half of it left, even after the drubbing he'd taken this evening. He'd spent too many nights outdoors on the cold hard autumn ground. He was rewarding himself.

He was just draining the last of his beer when the batwings opened behind him and the beefy Swede behind the bar said, "Not in here, miss. No ladies allowed."

"Whores would be all right, though, I'll bet."

Whoever she was, she had a mouth on her sharp as a bowie knife. Fargo just had to turn around and see what she looked like.

She was damned pretty, a sweet, slim little blonde all innocent of face though the splendor of her curves defied the innocence of the eyes and mouth. She wore a blue Western shirt stuffed into a pair of denims that were, in turn, stuffed into a pair of Texas boots. But for all her good looks, the most notable thing about her was the .45 she carried in her right hand.

"I'm looking for a man named Theo Mason," she said.

"The banker from Redburn?"

"That's the one."

"He was in earlier. You can probably find him at his hotel."

"Appreciate it."

The Swede glanced at Fargo, then back at the girl. "What's the gun for?"

"The gun is for none of your business."

"You got a smart mouth on you for somebody your age."

She laughed. "So I hear." She seemed to notice Fargo for the first time. "You from town here?"

"Passing through."

"Thought so. You look too smart to be a yokel like the rest of these fellas."

The Swede said, "Good thing you're a gal. Otherwise you'd be walkin' around with a couple black eyes. You don't go insultin' my town without fightin' me, I'll tell you that."

But she'd left her deep blue eyes on Fargo. "Maybe we'll meet up later. My name's Bonnie McLure."

Fargo shrugged.

The girl disappeared between the batwings.

"Now there's a handful," Fargo said.

The Swede grinned, wiped massive hands on his dirty white apron. "In more ways than one. You see those tits of hers?"

"Yeah, I guess I did happen to notice them once or twice."

"And a nice bottom, too. But you'd have to put up with that mouth of hers." He poured himself a shot and threw it down. "Wonder what she wants Theo Mason for."

"My guess is she wants to shoot him."

"That'd be my guess, too." The Swede called out to a man sitting at a table by himself. "Henry, get your ass over to the Hotel Royale. Ask for a Theo Mason. Tell him there's some gal lookin' for him. With a gun."

Henry, whose dusty clothes and ragged beard marked him as one of the many gold-crazed miners who'd come out here seeking a fortune, said, "You stand me to two drinks if I do?"

"I'll stand you to one."

"Two."

The Swede sighed. "You see the kind of crap I have to put up with, mister?"

Fargo smiled.

"Two drinks and I'll do it, Swede," Henry said.

"Two drinks it is," the Swede said amiably. "Now get going."

Fargo put his hat on, hitched up his gun belt and threw his saddlebags over his shoulder. Wind raced into the saloon, rattling the batwings. Nice night for a warm room with a warm bed.

He gave a little salute off the edge of his hat brim and walked outside. The town seemed respectful of the sheriff's curfew. A lone buggy was the only vehicle in sight. The other two saloons were already dark. Fargo headed west. That's where the hotels were located. The Excelsior promised the lowest rates. He didn't need a palace.

He thought of checking on his big Ovaro stallion. Sort of reassuring the animal that he hadn't deserted him. But the horse would be fine at the livery where he'd left him.

It was meant to be a scream but something muffled it.

Fargo was passing the mouth of an alley just as snowflakes began appearing with no warning at all. He was just huddling deeper into his jacket when the sound came from the moon-shadowed alley.

He stopped, peered into the darkness. At first he saw nothing but a few garbage cans and a couple of stray cats sniffing around a back porch for food.

The silhouette of the man became coupled with the silhouette of the woman as he dragged her from behind a small loading dock. The dark shape of the woman was easy enough to recognize. She was the girl in the saloon who'd been looking for the banker.

The man slapped her with enough force to knock her to her knees. Then he reached down and grabbed her by the hair and yanked her to her feet again. The second blow was even harder than the first. This time her scream came loud and clear.

So much for my nice warm bed, Fargo thought. At least for now.

He dumped his saddlebags on the street and started running into the narrow alleyway. He pulled his Colt from its holster as he increased his speed.

By the time he reached the pair, the girl was on her knees again and the man was about to slap her.

Fargo was there in time to grab the man's wrist with enough fury to damn near snap it in half. The man groaned and tried to grab on to Fargo with his free hand. But Fargo was too quick. His fist hit the man squarely on the jaw. The man fell over backward.

Fargo tended to the girl. He helped her up. "You all right?"

"He's no gentleman."

"What the hell's going on here, anyway?"

"Do you have to swear?"

Fargo smiled. "You come into a saloon where no ladies are allowed. You have a gun and you get smart-mouthed with the bartender. I guess I didn't figure you for having such delicate ears."

"I hate vulgarity."

"What happened to your gun?"

"I took it away from her," said the man who was just now getting to his feet. "Otherwise she would have killed me with it." He grasped his jaw with long fingers. "You could do all right for yourself in a boxing ring."

The man surprised Fargo. No anger in his voice, no anger on his moon-traced face. He even put his hand out. They shook. "I'm Theo Mason. This little hellcat is Bonnie McLure. We're having a disagreement."

"A lot more than a 'disagreement.' "

"I'm sure this man doesn't want to hear about our personal problems." To Fargo he said, "I shouldn't have hit her. But I got mad when she pulled the gun on me. I always get mad when I'm scared. I thought she was actually going to shoot me."

"I was going to, too, Theo."

Moonlight glinted off the .45 that lay next to the small loading dock. Fargo went over and picked it up. Looked to be the same gun she'd been toting in the saloon.

"I don't usually hit women."

"You sound like you deserve a medal."

Mason laughed. Though he was a dude in a three-piece suit, a boiled white shirt and a tan cravat to match the brown of his attire, there was a muscularity in his face and body that marked him as capable of defending himself. A lot of drunks had probably underestimated him, to their later dismay.

"You look like a man with a sense of humor. A medal for not hitting a woman. Did you hear that, Bonnie?"

"Yeah. Real funny."

Fargo looked from one to the other. "So am I through here?"

"He cheated on me."

"I'm too much of a gentleman to share some of her sins in public, Mr.—?"

"Fargo."

"Fargo, it is. Her father raised her to be a lady, but you can see that it didn't quite work out that way." Mason was mad now and had been ever since she'd brought up his cheating. Fargo figured Mason was right. None of this was Fargo's business. In fact, it was embarrassing to stand there and have to hear it.

He looked wistfully to the head of the alley. He just wanted to pick up his saddlebags and mosey over to the hotel.

"If you two try to kill each other later on, please leave me out of it, all right?"

Bonnie frowned. Mason laughed. "I'd feel the same way, Fargo. The same way exactly."

This was the first time Fargo had run into them together.

Unfortunately for him, it wouldn't be the last.

By the time he got to his hotel, Fargo was restless again. He found another card game in a room off the hotel taproom and sat in. No better luck this time than earlier in the evening.

After a couple hands, one of the older players said, "No way I'm lettin' that little gal sit in again."

"She shouldn't be allowed in here anyway," another said.

"I still say the only way she won was she cheated," a third offered.

"Cheated and used those nice sweet breasts of hers."

"Not to mention those big blue eyes."

By now, the men were laughing.

"She take you for a lot of money?" Fargo said.

"She sure did, mister."

"But we deserved it. We were watchin' her instead of our cards."

"Exactly what did she look like?" Fargo asked.

And, just as expected, the description he got fit perfectly the young woman he'd seen in the alley with Theo Mason. He'd seen Mason strike the girl but the girl didn't seem hurt. In fact, there was a feeling of ritual to the whole thing, as if this happened to the two of them many times over.

"You know her?" one of the players asked.

"Met her briefly."

"She's an eyeful, ain't she?"

"I'll give her that," Fargo said. "She's an eyeful, all right."

"She take you for any money?"

Fargo laughed. "She didn't have the time. Otherwise, she'd probably have my horse and saddle by now."

"Women like her are a menace to society," said the first man. "They always get their way by cheating."

"That's 'cause we're stupid enough to let 'em," said the second.

"They never get hanged, either," said the third man. "Knew a gal over to Denver. Opened up her husband's throat with a butcher knife while he was sleepin'. And what did she serve for it? Three years. Judge and jury said her old man didn't treat her right. Made her real nervous all the time, see, what with his temper and whatnot. So she served three years and they let her go. And guess what?"

"What?" said the first man.

"Couple years later she got herself another man and did the same damned thing all over again."

"Cut his throat?" the second man said.

"Ear to ear," said the storyteller.

"How much time did she serve for the second one?" the first man wanted to know.

"Take a guess," the storyteller said.

"Ten years?"

"Nope."

"Twenty?"

"Nope. Four years."

"Four years for doin' it a second time?"

Fargo pitched his cards and stood up. The boys were now more interested in talking than playing. But he'd learned one thing—the young woman he'd seen in the alley sure was some piece of work, slick, slippery, and probably dangerous as all hell.